Bernard Barker

Eliot the younger

A fiction in freehand

Bernard Barker

Eliot the younger
A fiction in freehand

ISBN/EAN: 9783337282400

Printed in Europe, USA, Canada, Australia, Japan

Cover: Foto ©Andreas Hilbeck / pixelio.de

More available books at **www.hansebooks.com**

ELIOT THE YOUNGER.

A Fiction in Freehand.

BY

BERNARD BARKER.

> " For several virtues
> Have I liked several women .   .   .   .
>   " Without the which, this story
> Were most impertinent."
>   *Tempest* (Act iii., sc. 1.—Act i., sc. 2.).

IN THREE VOLUMES.

VOL. II.

London:

SAMUEL TINSLEY & CO.,
10, SOUTHAMPTON STREET, STRAND.
1878.

CONTENTS OF VOL. II.

———∞⋆∞———

ELIOT THE YOUNGER.

CHAPTER I.

A SUNDAY OUT.

IN the early October Dick Eliot returned to Oxford; came home at Christmas; went back in March; and was once more released from his studies in July.

A portion of the Long Vacation he spent at the houses of certain of his fellow-collegians; the remainder with his own people. Another summer passed into another autumn,

and again Dick was at Oxford. The history
of this year, so far as it immediately concerns
our hero, we shall give in as few words as
may be.

In resuming his career as a student, after
the first break, it was with two distinct and
opposing influences at work within him, each
originating with a woman. Moreover, to
these two, as time passed, there had gradually
been added a third, also of feminine establish-
ment ; and thus, like some Hellenic hero of old,
Richard Eliot lived out his days beneath the
spell of the Fateful Three, whose names, erst
Clotho, Lachesis, and Atropos, were here
modernised into Lydia, Margaret, and Phœbe.

And first of Lydia—Mrs. Drummond, *née*
Brooke.

The rebuff to Dick's boyish passion for the
ex-governess, and the disillusions attending
thereon, had engendered in him a certain
spirit of revolt and recklessness, and had

fostered that perilous tendency to lawless excitement which was an inherent weakness of his nature. This spirit, as we have before hinted, had found early expression in his indulgence in dubious society, quasi-respectable pastimes, and the like.

Returning to Oxford, he had almost insensibly seceded from his former associates to another and faster set of men—a set that preferred billiards to boating; that studied cards (the devil's books), rather than those specially recommended by the authorities; that kept unholy hours (burning, not indeed the midnight oil, but the candle at both ends!) and inclining to what Lamb grimly calls "wet damnation." *Mais on peut tout pardonner à la jeunesse.* "The passions of youth," says Longfellow, "like unhooded hawks, fly high. They are musical with bells upon their jesses, and we forget the cruelty of the sport in the dauntless bearing of the gallant bird." Which, *en passant*, is a pretty enough piece of sophistry, but scarcely what one would have expected from the pen of a professor.

As a set-off against this unfortunate impulsion to evil which possessed our hero, there was the remembrance of Margaret Oglevie. The influence her words and example exercised over his mind was an altogether pure and elevating one, and the thought of her frank, virginal eyes, her gracious speech, and gentle loyalty of regard, was an ever-recurring check and reproach to him in the perverse course of his backsliding. Always prone to idealise, Dick Eliot had made Margaret to typify for him the higher life his better nature aspired to. His feeling for her was a complex one, made up of simple reverence for her goodness, gratitude for the help, actual and imaginary, he got from her, and a profound admiration of her intellect. He acknow-

ledged her his superior in every respect, as
well mentally as morally. His belief in her
was unbounded; she became one of his
cherished articles of faith; and pursuing his
literary loves and ambitions, he seldom
penned a line or stanza without secretly
thinking of her as his critic, without hoping
her approval, fearing her condemnation.

But although the spirit was thus willing to
be worthy her approbation, the flesh was
most wofully weak. Again and again, seeking his ghostly couch in the still small
hours, after a night of many bumpers, of
high play, of chaotic folly, he would vow to
give up sack and live cleanly, as a gentleman
should; and again and again would cards be
dealt, corks be drawn, and money squandered.
The hackneyed Ovidian confession — *video
meliora proboque, deteriora sequor*—might
well have been made his own; for mortal
rarely at once respected and relinquished,

looked up to and fell away from virtue, so uniformly as he.

The third and more recent influence we have referred to, as bearing upon our young Oxonian at this stage of his existence, was that of Phœbe Langham, billiard-marker at the Goose and Gridiron.

Someone—Byron, we believe—argues that

" that's sincerest
Which is most acted on by what is nearest ; "

and Dick was certainly one over whom persons present were apt to exercise a greater sway than friends at a distance. He was one, too, who, like the unfortunate Captain Macheath, found female intercourse, in some shape or other, a necessity—("I must have women," cries Gay's graceless hero ; " there's nothing relaxes the mind like them !")—and thus the blue eyes and easy, enterprising tongue of Miss Langham were soon found a sufficient attraction to take him, at idle moments, to

Abingdon, where the girl had gradually got
to look for his coming, and would welcome
him as she welcomed none other of her real
or professed admirers. In justice to both,
young man and maiden, it must be recorded
that, for the present at least, neither had a
thought of possible harm resulting from their
acquaintance. A liking for each other's
society had sprung up, and they simply
obeyed the natural prompting of youthful
preference. How far their acquaintance had
ripened into intimacy may haply be gathered
from the recital of the following interview*
which took place one early October morning
at the close of the twelvemonth we are now
chronicling.

It was a Sabbath morning, silent and sun-
flooded. The air was unusually warm for the
time of year, and so Phœbe Langham sat at
the open window of the little inn-parlour—a
window that looked out upon the street. The

week's work was over; her uncle still lingered in bed, sleeping off his Saturday
night's potations; she had a new number of
the *Family Herald* to read, and until one
o'clock nothing was likely to prevent her
from following her own devices undis-
turbed.

Hence she took possession of the easiest
chair she could find, placed her feet upon a
second, and began to absorb her weekly
instalment of romance. Presently there came
the need of getting overleaf to an uncut
page, wherefore, by way of paper-knife,
Phœbe produced from her pocket a certain
stout playing-card—sole relic of a pack left
by a stray party of collegians one rainy afternoon at the Goose and Gridiron. The card
was the ace of clubs, or, as Phœbe *naïvely*
described it, " the one of shamrocks." With
this she proceeded to sever her paper; and it
was whilst thus occupied at the window that

the church-going public began passing by on its way to morning service.

Morality, we know, is greatly dependent upon geography. What, for instance, is perfectly innocent in the South Sea Islands, is perfectly scandalous in the British, for the social latitude allowed one mainly varies with the mundane longitude one lives in. And this difference in the popular estimate of what is right and wrong extends to places probably farther apart even than those we have cited, inasmuch as the general conduct of the occupants of heaven, were it imitated here below, would doubtless be condemned by the dwellers upon earth as indelicate. And thus (to come to an individual case), although in some happy climes Phœbe Langham might have sat, novel-reading, on two chairs at an open window, without offence—might have taken her ease at her inn on a Sunday morning *sans peur et sans reproche*—it was certainly not to be tolerated in Christian England.

The people passed. Like wind-waves over a cornfield swept their shadows across the page that Phœbe was reading ; but she was all too engrossed in the fortunes of fictitious men and maidens to heed the sterner realities of the world without. Not so these. Mrs. Grundy, sailing, silk-clad, to her devotions, turned eyes of unutterable disapproval on the unconscious damsel as she rustled by, directing the attention of her eldest daughter to the heinous spectacle ; whereat Miss Grundy shuddered so emphatically that, being strait-laced, something abruptly and audibly snapped in twain. Anon came Mrs. Grundy's friends and neighbours, and each, in passing, clutched tighter her prayer-book, and was censoriously aware of Phœbe and her *Family Herald*, of her lifted legs and the ace of clubs. It was Philistia reviewing Bohemia—the proprieties (those Eumenides, daughters of Earth!) taking stock of the unenthralled.

After a while the shadows moving by became fewer, the bells ceased ringing, the street was silent. For half-an-hour no sound was heard save the voices of some truant children in the neighbouring churchyard, and the twitter of sparrows on the housetop. Then arose certain other notes, notes which did not belong to the birds. It was someone whistling—whistling not loudly or assertively, but in a key clearly audible through the prevailing quiet—and by-and-by there appeared round the street-corner Dick Eliot.

As he approached the Goose and Gridiron, his whistling gradually softened, finally dying away altogether. A minute or so he lingered to adjust his loosely-knotted necktie, to settle his straw boating-hat fairly on his head, and generally to "pull himself together." Then he went on with a quickened

step, well nigh passing the window at which
Phœbe Langham was seated before he perceived her.   He halted abruptly, but Phœbe
still remained unconscious of his presence.
Seeing this, he gently moved away to the
arched entry leading to the inn-yard, whence
a side door conducted one into the house.   By
this means he made his way to the little front
parlour, on the threshold of which he paused.

"Is that you, Mary Ann?" said Phœbe,
without, however, turning her head, and still
endeavouring to maintain her attention on
the story she was reading.   "I wish you'd
see if my things have come home from the
wash yet.   They ought to have been brought
yesterday, by rights; and last night I dreamt
that that old wretch of a washerwoman had
stolen my best dimity!   Just look—there's
a dear!"

"Certainly I will, if you ask so prettily,"
said Dick, coming forward.

" My goodness *gracious!*—what's that " exclaimed Phœbe, springing to her feet, and wheeling sharply round. " Why, Mis-ter Eliot, I declare ! And I thought it was cook! Only fancy ! But how are you ? You look seedy—what's the matter ?"

" Oh, I'm all right enough. Mixed a little too much, perhaps, at Tyndall's supper last night. That's the worst of me ; I always mix. Confound the drink ! I wish it were at Jericho !"

" People wouldn't want to be told to go there if it was," said Phœbe ; then, gravely looking down, with a rather heightened colour, " I don't like that Mr. Tyndall ; and if I was you——"

" Well—if you were me ?"

" Never mind. I was going to say something ; but I shan't. Tell me, how is it you're in Abingdon ? Why ain't you at church or something ?"

"Not up to it. Thought I'd make some excuse to have a walk instead, and shake off my headache. You know the song:

'I take me a stroll for the sake of my soul;
   Church-goer, the dickens is in it,
If you get as much good from the drone of the priest
   As I from the song of the linnet!'"

"Linnet!" echoed Phœbe, her country breeding involuntarily asserting itself. "Why, you wouldn't hear any linnet at this time of the year! Plenty of snipe, and woodcock, and wild duck, and that sort of thing about; but then, of course, they don't sing. And even if they did, I s'pose you couldn't well bring 'em into poetry—not like larks and linnets, you know? Could you?"

"Oh, I don't know. Get 'em in somehow," said Dick, with a fine show of careless confidence. "But where's the governor? I want some beer. I'm a traveller, you know; so you're bound to let me have it."

"I'll draw you some. Uncle's in bed, as usual; and aunt's away at Reading. There's been no one in the house but Mary Ann nearly all the week—Mary Ann and me. And you haven't been over to see us once!"

So saying, the girl reached down a jug from an upper shelf, and quitted the room without turning her face to Dick ere she went. Left to himself, our hero mechanically took up the paper Phœbe had thrown aside, and glanced at the tale she had been reading. It was the usual thing—the old, old story— a vulgarised version of King Cophetua, or of the Lord of Burleigh. A titled wooer and a low-born maiden; triumph of true love, and defeat of what Mr. Yellowplush calls "the villain's McHinations!" Dick fell a-musing. He was feeling fagged with the monotony of ill-spent hours, worried with increasing debts and entanglements, which he shrank from confessing to his father. A sense of reaction was upon him; and, conscious of a temporary distaste for evil, he believed himself possessed of a permanent relish for good—which, by-the-way, is a very common error among men.

In his existing state of mind, Dick felt a longing for rest and retirement, surcease from excitement, and a craving for cool grasses and the quiet sky. As a step toward simplicity and comparative innocence, he had now requested a draught of homely malt, in place of the wonted extravagance of soda-and-brandy. Phœbe brought it him in a tankard, and then resumed her seat at the window. She did not, however, again extend her feet to a second chair, but instead thereof curled one leg deftly under her, whilst letting the other swing idly to and fro like a pendulum. She leaned an elbow on the window-sill; and, thus disposed, prepared to attend her visitor.

For some minutes there was silence between

them. Dick kept a lingering hold on his pewter, gazing thoughtfully into its depths, as he tilted it toward him. Phœbe absently inserted a small brown finger in the hole in the sill that received the shutter-bolt, at the bottom whereof lay a last year's cherry-stone, which had long defied her efforts to extract it. Dick eventually spoke.

"Well, Phœbe! you don't seem particularly pleased to see a fellow now he *has* come."

"Oh, indeed! Is that what a fellow thinks?"

"Yes, it is. Don't see how he's to think otherwise."

"H'm!" said Phœbe, with tightened lips; then after a momentary pause, "How d'ye liké our new beer?"

"Beer's all right enough. Why do you ask? Same tap as before, I suppose?"

No answer.

"I suppose it's the same tap as before?"
persisted Dick, looking toward his companion,
whose head was bowed over the window-
sill.

Still no answer.

"Have I offended you?" asked Dick,
abruptly pushing away his pewter, and
drawing nearer to her. "Why, Phœbe!
Whatever is the matter? You're crying!"

"No, I'm not."

"I beg pardon."

"Yes, I am. But it's nothing—nothing
at all! I—I can't get this beastly cherry-
stone out of the hole here, and it—it worries
me!"

"I see," said Dick, gently. "It *is* provoking, that sort of thing—awful! Let me have
a try at the beggar."

And, with the natural delicacy of a gentleman, he straightway turned his attention
exclusively to the task in question, thereby

giving Phœbe time to recover her self-command.

The girl hastily brushed the tears from her eyes, went to the sideboard and placed awry a row of tankards hitherto in order, then came back to the window.

" It's no use," exclaimed Dick ; "it's not to be got out at any price. You see the hole is too deep and narrow."

" Never mind, Mr. Eliot."

" All right ! I don't, if you don't. Where are you going this afternoon ?"

" This afternoon ? Nowhere."

" It's a glorious day ! Couldn't you contrive to get away a little while ? Come as far as Nuneham with me in my boat. I brought something to carry two, on purpose."

" Did you, though ? Ah, I should like !"

" Then come ! Mary Ann can manage alone, can't she ?"

"Oh, yes; she could manage alone well enough. But——"

"But what? I'm off to the hotel now, to see about some dinner. I shall look for you at the lock between two and three. Say you'll come, Phœbe?"

The girl's face flushed, and her eyes sought the ground.

"If I can I will," she answered, in a low voice.

"That's famous! Now good-bye, then—till this afternoon!"

And, with this, he went.

*   *   *   *   *

Twilight was creeping over the land when Dick and Phœbe returned from their afternoon excursion. Side by side they traversed the dim stretch of meadow-land that lay between Abingdon lock and the town, the grey, mist-veiled river gliding stealthily by on their right, the voices of rooks in their nesting-trees coming solemnly toward them from the farmstead to the left.

A faint touch of frost was in the air; a thin ghostly vapour wandered across the fields; but the stars twinkled clear and cold in the sky overhead, and here and there home-lights gleamed brightly from the town.

Phœbe's arm was drawn within her companion's, her hand held in his; and ever and again as some low-flitting owl sailed by them, with its forlorn, half-human cry, or the unseen web of the gossamer-spider floated across their faces, the girl pressed closer to his side.

It had been a memorable afternoon for both. They had landed at Nuneham, had strolled through the autumn woods, taken tea at the keeper's cottage (where Dick was known to the occupants), and had become foolishly, fondly, perilously confidential in their intercourse.

Phœbe had owned to Dick the growing unbearableness of her situation, had shed not a few tears, and had talked wildly of running away from Abingdon, and seeking her fortune in London.

Here, she explained, lived an aunt—a box-keeper, or something of the sort, at one of the theatres—and, although she knew but little of this relative, she felt that her lot, under any conditions, could scarce be worse than at present.

For a while she seemed inconsolable ; but an inconsolable woman (as we have some-where read) is simply a woman in want of consolation. This Dick, to the best of his ability, administered. He could nor bear to see the girl cry, and, moved by her emotion —and his own—he probably said considerably more, and acted otherwise, than his cooler reason would have dictated. In fine, the pair lost their heads utterly, becoming so ripe for ruin, that, had they, instead of the original man and woman, been the tenants of Eden, we verily believe the serpent would have had a sinecure.

CHAPTER II.

"PARTANT POUR LA SYRIE."

THE next day Dick Eliot came over to Abingdon to fetch his boat, which he had left, under charge, in the shed at the lock.

He came by road, being driven by his friend Teddy Swift—a gentleman whose passion for tandem was so notorious and engrossing, that once, when up for examination, he was recorded to have translated *os frontis*, " the fore horse." So, at least, said Dick ; but we rather suspect this to have been an invention of his own.

Our hero called at the Goose and Gridiron,

and had speech with Phœbe Langham. She
looked pale and languid, as though suffering
from lack of sleep, and greeted him with a
timidity that was new to her. Each, at first,
was somewhat constrained in manner. Presently, however, Mr. Swift appeared, and the
conversation became more easy.

"Hullo, Phœbekins !" cried that lively
young gentleman, accosting her. " How do
the hermetically sealed antipathies of the
Holy Grail agree with your diabolical consti-
tution ? I mean, *comment se va-t-il ?*"

Miss Langham smiled, and intimated that
she was perfectly well—an assertion her looks
belied.

After tarrying an hour, both gentlemen
arose to depart, Dick intending to return by
the river, whilst his friend took the road.
The former lingered a moment to whisper a
few parting words to Phœbe in the passage.
There was not much in them, but the girl

seemed grateful that they should have been spoken.

Walking away together, Mr. Swift quoth to Mr. Eliot :

" Young man, you're a-going of it !"

" What do you mean ?" said Dick, flushing up.

" Nothing," answered Mr. Swift, closing one eye in a low and vulgar manner. " Nothing whatsumdever !"

" Then why do you wink in that disgusting way ? Really, Ted, you are quite insufferable sometimes, and I'm sure, if I hadn't the temper of an angel——"

("Of an angel ! O crumbs !" interjected Mr. Swift.)

"——I shouldn't be able to stand it. If you've anything to say, let's hear it and have done with it."

" All right ; here goes, then ! Chuck up card-playing with Tyndall's lot ; don't

patronise that hell-hole in Thingamy Street
so often ; cut drink ; smoke less ; study a
little more ; and keep clear of Abingdon for a
while. No business of mine, of course ; but
happening to be passing, and that sort o'
thing, I thought I'd just mention it."

For a second or so Dick bit his lip, and
looked as black as thunder. Mr. Swift gazed
blandly into vacancy, whistling mellifluously.
Then, on a sudden, Dick's face relaxed. He
held forth his hand, and grasped that of his
comrade with nervous fervour.

" Oh, Ted !" he groaned, " I'm such a fool !
I've got into an infernal groove, somehow,
and I seem daily going from bad to worse. I
can't sleep at night for thinking of the
morrow ! I shall never face my exam.—
never ! I'm head and ears in debt, and—
well ! there'll be the very devil to pay before
long !"

" Tell your governor, Dick ; he'll pay him."

"Dear old dad! Ted, I *dare* not; he's been so good to me! No; I shall enlist, or go off to Australia, or do something desperate —that's what it'll be; you see if it isn't. Good-bye, old boy."

"Eh! I say! You ain't off now, are you? not to Australia, you know? None of your larks!"

"No, no," said Dick, smiling, in spite of himself, at Swift's anxious look of distrust. "It's all right. See you to-night. Bye-bye!"

    *   *   *   *   *

Just three weeks after the foregoing conversation, on the first day of the month of November, there happened at the College of St. Sepulchre an event which, for the time being, made that venerable institution a bye-word and a reproach in the mouths of the University authorities—a name of evil odour in the nostrils of dean and don, doctor and proctor. Mr. Marmaduke Tyndall gave a party, a party which achieved a greatness (unpremeditated, indeed) second only to that of the renowned Hans Breitmann. And there were present at the ceremony, *cum multis aliis*, Mr. Richard Eliot and his fellow-student, Edward Swift.

The latter had at first declined to accept the invitation extended him ; but, on Dick's representing that the affair was to be nothing more than a friendly celebration of their host's birthday ("just a glass of grog and a quiet rubber"), and not, as was too often the case, a riotous gathering of gamblers and wine-bibbers, Mr. Smith had consented to assist.

"The ways of Providence," says Mrs. Malaprop, "are unscrupulous!"

How was it that Mr. Tyndall's party, honestly meant to be of the mildest, the most harmless and rational, should have resulted in the awful orgie and saturnalia it did, was a thing no man was ever able clearly to explain. What wand of Comus waved above their heads, what wicked spells cast into the "spongy air" of Mr. Tyndall's rooms, should have transformed a dozen decent young Englishmen into a drove of wild, ungovernable animals, and the college quad into a waste howling wilderness, where night was made hideous with firearms and fireworks, breaking crockery, and Bacchanalian chorus —this was more than human tongue might tell.

Rack-punch on the top of bottled stout was clearly insufficient to account for any such outcome ; nor could the simple round of champagne that followed be fairly cited as an accessory. The secret of mischief was evidently of deeper, of subtler origin.

Our task, now, however, is to deal with the consequences, not with the causes of the outbreak ; nor do we purpose giving fuller details of the eruption itself. Suffice to say that, on the morrow, ten or twelve rioters were haled before the authorities ; were first examined by the proctor, and subsequently handed over to the inquisitors of the common room, where the Master, the Bursar, the Dean, and half-a-dozen tutors were found ranged in a terrible row to confront them. These gentlemen unanimously pronounced the proceedings of the previous night to have been of so unprecedented, so outrageous, so egregious a character, that the most prompt, stringent, and decisive example must obviously be made of the offending parties. Messrs. Tyndall and Eliot, convicted as ringleaders (it was Tyndal who had discharged the revolver, whilst Dick had been the artist in fireworks), were sentenced to rustication for a year, the remaining transgressors being condemned to a variety of lesser pains

and penalties for their share in the shindy,
or, in Proctorian phrase, their participation in
the disturbance.

Rustication for a year! So this was the
end of it—this was what it had come to!
" Non-university men sneer at rustication,"
says a well-known writer; " they can't see
any particular punishment in having to absent
one's self from one's studies for a term or two.
But do they think that the Dons don't know
what they are about? Why, nine spirited
young fellows out of ten would snap their
fingers at rustication, if it wasn't for the *home*
business. It is breaking the matter to the
father, his just anger, and the mother's still
more bitter reproaches. It must all come out,
the why and the wherefore, without conceal-
ment or palliation. The college write a letter
to justify themselves, and then a mine of
deceit is sprung under the parents' feet, and
their eyes are opened to things they little

dreamt of. This, it appears, is not the first offence. The college has been long-suffering, and has pardoned when it should have punished repeatedly. The lad who was thought to be doing so well has been leading a dissipated, riotous life, and deceiving them all. This is the bitterest blow they have ever had. How can they trust him again? And so the wound takes long to heal, and sometimes is never healed at all. That is the meaning of rustication."

An hour Dick Eliot passed alone in his room, a confusion of bills and papers on the table before him. With a dazed notion of facing the difficulty, a faint hope that things might not be so bad, after all, as he fancied, he strove to form some accurate estimate of his position; but, with a head swimming, a hand shaking, from his last night's wassail, and the stunned sensation which follows any sudden adverse stroke of fate, all calculation

seemed impossible to him.   By-and-by he
took from his locker in the window-seat a
flask of brandy.   He poured some into a wine-
glass, and swallowed it neat.   Its effect was
to steady his nerves somewhat, and to help
him in the resolution which was already half-
formed in his heart.

Hastily sweeping up the litter of docu-
ments that represented his debts to tailor and
bootmaker, wine merchant and tobacconist,
bookseller, boat-builder, livery stables, and
the like—he crammed them pell-mell into his
desk, taking therefrom a sheet or two of note-
paper, ere he locked it and put it aside.   Then
he sat him down, and, with bent brow and
set teeth, and much bitter groaning of spirit,
proceeded to indite a couple of letters, the
first of which he addressed to Oscar Dale,
Esq., Idlewild, near Hethercote, Norfolk; the
second to Miss Langham, Goose and Gridiron,
Abingdon.

No. 1 was a confession. It told of folly, and punishment, and penitence. It was written in alternate accents of despondency and desperation, as the sense of his situation, or the stimulant he had taken, came uppermost; as *atra cura*, or curaçoa, asserted itself. It implored its recipient to break the matter to his parents. It expressed, in no measured and not unmanly terms, a sense of shame for past misconduct; and it concluded as follows :

" By the time you get this I shall be out of Oxford. I intend starting for London to-night. What I shall do there remains to be proved ; but, happen what will, I am deter-mined not again to face friends and family until, in some way or other, I have retrieved my character. I'm rusticated for a year—and by Heaven, Dale, I'll work out that year by myself. Ask my dear father to forgive me. Tell my mother not to be uneasy about me ;

and let no one attempt to seek me out.   Bid
them all think as kindly of me, dear Dale, as
they can ; and believe me now, as ever,
sincerely yours,

" RICHARD ELIOT."

Epistle No. 2 was briefer, and in reality
had no particular *raison d'être.*   It apprised
Phœbe, with tragic terseness, of the Nemesis
that had overtaken him, and told her of the
course he had decided to adopt.   It intimated
that the writer was sternly resolved to do or
die.   It promised to communicate anew with
her at an early date (" as soon as I have
looked about me, and arranged my plans,")
and, meanwhile, bade her wear the ring
enclosed for his sake, and try not wholly to
forget her unhappy and affectionate friend,
Dick.

These letters written, and our hero thereby
pledged to a definite course of action, he

experienced a sense of considerable relief. Indeed, such is the elasticity of youth, its zest for adventure, and its confidence in its own resources, that he looked forward to the coming change with secret impatience, and a feeling almost of elation. Eager, moreover, to consummate his indiscretion, he sought to get the two missives posted without delay. Leaning from his window, which overlooked the quadrangle, he presently caught sight of a passing acquaintance.

"Below there!" cried he.

The person thus hailed naturally gazed in every direction but the right one, ere his wandering vision discovered Dick.

"I say! You're not going near the post-office, are you?"

"Yes, I am. What do you want?"

"Just post these letters for me, there's a brick—two of 'em. *Catch!*"

And down they fluttered into the college-cap held out for them, the owner of which was pleased to remark that that was what *he* called " dropping a line to a friend."

"And, Eliot, old chap," continued the man, "I'm jolly sorry about your rustication, you know. Awful hard lines, and no mistake! But then, you did come it rather strong—didn't you, now? Jove! it *must* have been a lark! When do you go home, old boy?"

"Not going home; somewhere else," said Dick, sententiously, and nodding to his interlocutor, he closed the window and withdrew.

Now it happened that the man who had taken charge of our hero's correspondence was one Tom Towle, a nephew of the reverend gentleman whose wife was erewhile introduced to the reader at Norwich, at the house of Ralph Oglevie. And before putting the letters in the post he glanced, with pardonable curiosity, at their superscriptions. And when he had read the address to Miss Langham he whistled. For Eliot's intimacy with this young lady had lately given rise to a good deal of uncharitable remark among a certain set of Oxford men, of which set it chanced that Mr. Towle was one. Wherefore he now looked upon Dick's epistle with the cold eye of suspicion—suspicion that after events fully confirmed in his mind : of which more anon.

Dick's next step, having got rid of his letters, was to pack a portmanteau and send it to the station. This done, he released from the coal-cupboard under the stairs his little black terrier Satan (a wiry, rough-and-tumble quadruped, recently purchased of old Joe Langham, Phœbe's uncle, and a favourite of her own), and sallied forth on a call of condolence upon Tyndall. He found that worthy in his rooms, slightly intoxicated, and surrounded by half-a-dozen fellow-victims of the yesternight's escapade, on all of whom sentence of rustication, for longer or shorter terms, had been passed. Dick ("one more unfortunate!") was greeted with effusion. He was invited to join in making up a farewell dinner-party, to take place that evening at the Crown and Sceptre; and, this invitation being accepted, he found himself, some few hours after, eating the last meal he was destined to consume as an Oxford undergraduate.

What the banquet was like may, perhaps, be more easily imagined than described. (We love to use a set phrase, such as this, now and again; it revives the reader's confidence.) From being preternaturally dull at the beginning it became preternaturally lively at the end. Dick, however, having a special object in view, maintained a sobriety above the average; and when, at about eleven p.m., the party broke up, he shook hands heartily all round, and turned his face toward the railway station. But he was not to be parted with thus lightly ; for Mr. Tyndall, affectionately backed up by little Charley Vaughan, insisted on seeing him " safely off the premises."

Half-an-hour later, when the 11. 30 to town went creaking and shrieking from under the echoing roof of the dim-lit station, disappearing amidst a cloud of angry smoke along the dark, misty line, two great-coated gentlemen remained on the deserted platform, gazing pensively after it.

" Farewell, Brutus ; we shall meet at Philippi," said the taller of the two, apostrophising the now invisible train, to the drowsy admiration of a passing porter. " He's gone Charley—gone from my gaze like a beautiful dream ; ' and there is nothing left remarkable beneath the visiting moon !' "

"Dick was very drunk," said the second, in a moralising tone, nipping a hiccough in the bud.

"Oh, awful!" agreed his friend. "So are you, Charley! So am I—disgracefully drunk! And——Hullo! Is it a porter that I see before me? Porter, I'll play you chess or hunt - the - slipper for a sovereign; and Vaughan (you know Vaughan), Vaughan shall be umpire—won't you, Vaughan?"

"Oh, bother; Let's go to bed! Come along, old fellow!"

"Happy thought, Charley! So we will. Porter, adieu! God bless you! Be good, and you'll be happy.

'Now will I to my couch, although to rest
Is almost wronging such a night as this!'

Cats and codfish! how it's raining!"

*   *   *   *   *

As, in City circles, one firm seldom "goes" but another quickly follows (there

having been private ties and transactions
between the two); or as, in the familiar
avalanche of the fireside, the poker rarely
falls without bringing down the tongs also ;
so, in like unlucky sequence, Dick Eliot's
disappearance was followed by that of Phœbe
Langham.

When the girl read the letter Dick had
written her (on the evening of the day it
was despatched), she was filled with distress.
Perhaps it were hardly fair to inquire too
closely as to the dreams she had dreamt
concerning our hero ; but, whatsoever these
may have been, her feeling for the subject of
them was a genuinely warm one. Indeed,
her heart had really been touched by his
attentions, by his invariable gentleness and
consideration, and by the partiality he had
expressed for her. She wept many tears
over the tidings of his untoward fortune, and
the thought of the possible trials in store for

him awakened her liveliest sympathy and concern.

Alone in London! *Alone?* And why should he be alone? Why should not she go thither also, as, in her heart, she had so repeatedly vowed she would? The hot young blood came tingling tumultuously back into her pale cheeks at the idea. Yes, she would go, too; would quit for ever her hateful drudgery at the tavern: would seek out her dead mother's sister, and implore her for counsel and protection! Ere long, moreover, she would surely fall in with Richard Eliot—(her notions of London were of the vaguest)—and all she asked, all she yearned for, was just to look upon his face once again!

Throughout the night Phœbe lay awake, revolving her plans and prospects; and at earliest dawn, gathering together in a bundle a few simple belongings, and leaving a brief line of farewell behind her, she stole from out the sleeping house into the foggy darkness of the November morning, hurriedly making her way to the station.

That same day the news of her flight reached Oxford. (A party of St. Sepulchre men had been over to Abingdon and brought the intelligence back with them.) Then it was that Tom Towle, putting this and that together, and mindful of the missive he had posted, was inspired with the idea of coupling her departure with that of our hero. The notion, once started, was widely debated ; an accumulation of minor accidents, of casual evidence, was adduced in support of the Towlean theory ; and presently it was generally asserted, and as generally believed, that Phœbe Langham ("girl at the Goose and Gridiron, you know !") had gone off to London with Eliot of Sepulchre's.

CHAPTER III.

WHAT THE WORLD SAID.

"A GIRL that whistles, and wears no stays!"

The speaker was Mrs. Towle; the scene the drawing-room at The Coppice. And the vicar's wife held in her hand a letter (bearing the Oxford postmark), to which she now referred.

"They are my nephew's identical words, received by Mr. Towle only yesterday. 'A girl that whistles—that whistles (oh, here it is!)—that whistles and wears no stays!' Speaks volumes, *that* does! And she was billiard-sharper at the — the Goose of

Gideon! At least, it looks like the Goose of Gideon; but Tom's a regular Towle, and can no more write plainly than his poor father could. Dreadful business, isn't it? Upon my word, I wonder what next! First young Drummond, and now young Eliot— why, it's—it's abominable!"

"I don't believe one half of it!" cried a clear voice, with a little thrill of indignation in it.

"Gracious, Maggie! I'd no idea you were there, or I shouldn't have spoken. I'm sure it's not a fit subject to discuss before a young girl, and I shall never so much as mention the misguided youth before my Sophia again. I quite understand your not believing it, my dear child; it's to your credit you don't. But, then, you haven't learnt the wickedness of the world, as I and your good father have. And Mrs. Cundy here, of course!"

Saying which, Mrs. Towle hastily made an

apologetic half-turn toward her elderly relative, to intimate that she was included, as an equal with Mr. Oglevie and herself, in their acquaintance with evil.

"Ah!" sighed the widowed one; "and that's true, too! I've seen a deal of iniquity in my time; as much as my betters. And since my poor Joseph went to heaven——"

"It's what we must all come to," broke in Mrs. Towle, dogmatically—(as who should look upon heaven as Hobson's choice, awkward but unavoidable)—"and I'm sure the things one has to put up with here below are enough—enough——"

"To make a saint swear," suggested Ralph Oglevie, grimly contracting his bushy grey eyebrows. "Well, Mrs. Towle! I agree with you that it's a foolish business—a very foolish business; but I also agree with Maggie, and believe no more than half I hear."

"But my *dear* Mr. Oglevie," exclaimed

the vicar's helpmate, in peremptory tones, "it's the talk of the whole place! Besides, here's Tom's letter!"

"Tom of Oxford," quoth Mr. Oglevie, coolly, "is possibly at fault. I don't mean to say that your nephew hasn't a perfect right to repeat the common rumour—the popular belief about the affair; but then popular belief is so often popular error. The lad has been rusticated, sure enough (I saw Dale last night, and had a talk with him touching our young friend); but what of that? Most likely it was a wholesale conspiracy on the part of the Dons. Those Dons, ma'am, are very Catilines at scheming. They were, I recollect, when I was at college. Yes; just so!"

Thus speaking, Ralph Oglevie rose from his seat, took snuff with determination, and addressed himself to his favourite indoor exercise of pacing the chamber from end to end, his hands loosely clasped behind him. This practice he was wont to pursue, wholly irrespective of the room or company in which he might find himself.

Mrs. Towle followed him with impatient eyes as he went, with measured steps, the length of the apartment; and, when he turned and approached her anew, she prepared once more to assert herself.'

"Pray, Mr. Oglevie, if you doubt this report about the girl (which seems more than probable to *me*, mind you !), what do you say to the young gentleman's debts ? there's no mistake about *them !* Eleven hundred pounds, if you please ; and near two hundred of that, Mrs. Cundy, for wines and cigars ! Think of it !"

"Eleven hundred ?" said Mr. Oglevie, abruptly pausing in his promenade. "That's a coincidence ! Shows how history repeats itself. Eleven hundred, Maggie, was what

your uncle Digby let us in for the year he
and I were at Christchurch together. Well,
well! there's nothing new under the sun—
unless," added the speaker, resuming his
walk, "it's iced coffee, polo, co-respondents,
and such like products of an advanced
civilisation."

Mrs. Towle began to lose temper. She had
called in upon the Oglevies a full hour earlier
than was customary, with the express intention
of astounding and confounding them with the
intelligence of Richard Eliot's enormities; but,
save for Margaret's momentary protest, her
news had been received with an *insouciance*,
an absence of moral susceptibility, and the
due expression of condemnation, that struck
her as being little short of indecent! Her
acquaintance with Ralph Oglevie was one of
many years'· standing ; and it was a constant
source of irritation to her, of secret mortifica-
tion, that she—an acknowledged power in

21—2

the parish—(riding roughshod, indeed, over the submissive majority of her husband's flock) should so signally fail to affect the owner of The Coppice. Mrs. Towle was by nature a bully—and of all bullies a woman-bully is the most cruel, the most cowardly! —and, finding so cool, so unshaken a front opposed to her, her heart became faint within her. Wherefore she strove to hide her sinking courage with additional bluster.

"Mr. Oglevie, I really do wish you'd sit down a minute while I'm talking to you, like an ordinary person! I can't help telling you, —but that stalking backward and forward of yours is most distracting. How *can* one converse comfortably with a man who is all over the room, like a Jack hare—first in one place, then in another?"

"Ah, yes, yes! we are here to-day and gone to-morrow," interjected the elderly relative, in a woolly aside.

"Come and walk *with* me, Mrs. Towle," said Mr. Oglevie, composedly; "it'll do you good. It's a famous habit to get into, too. At billiards, you know, one is calculated to do two miles in the hour; but at this sort of thing I consider I manage nearer three. Besides, we can't play billiards always, and we *can* get this."

Mrs. Towle looked indignant. Margaret, with her quick sense of humour, could scarce forbear smiling, picturing to herself the vicar's wife pacing beside her father up and down the drawing-room, or zealously coasting round a billiard-table. And subsequently, for her private amusement, she made a little pen-and-ink sketch of Mr. Oglevie as Marc Antony, and Mrs. Towle as Cleopatra, with the quotation, "Let us to billiards!" written beneath it.

But now Mrs. Towle was fairly roused to wrath, and the vials thereof were poured forth upon the head of our unlucky hero, who became the scapegoat of her ruffled humour. She denounced him *ex cathedrâ*, as it were ; almost putting him under the ban of the Church, and barely stopping short of excommunication. No words, in her opinion, were too strong to describe the unpardonable wickedness of his conduct. And then, in a strain common to a certain professedly pious class of persons, she spoke of the dealings of Providence with such sinners, of the assured punishment awaiting them, quoting divers Old Testament texts in which all the fanatical cruelty of ancient Judaism seemed concentrated. Here, however, noting his daughter's flush of pain and indignation, Ralph Oglevie interposed.

" Providence, Mrs. Towle," said he, sternly, " is actuated, I think, by a more Christian spirit than you appear disposed to credit it with. I should be sorry to hold the kind of views you have just pronounced of the mercy which endureth for ever. Such doctrine makes one inclined, in all reverence, to declare that it isn't the devil only, but God, who is not so black as he's painted! Let us change the subject, ma'am."

So serious, so severe and uncompromising, were the tones of the speaker, that, for once, at least, in her life, Mrs. Towle was effectually cowed. She muttered a half-audible word or two to herself, hastily collected her unattached belongings (such as her umbrella, her hand-bag, and the elderly relative), and therewith took her departure, a vanquished and crestfallen woman.

    *   *   *   *   *

At five o'clock there was afternoon service at the Cathedral, where Margaret Oglevie was a frequent attendant. To-day, as soon as Mrs. Towle had gone, she hastened to put on hat and cloak, and set out for The Close

—a good half-hour's walk from The Coppice.
She was feeling depressed and unhappy; her
heart seemed heavy within her breast; a
sense of emptiness and hopelessness had
come upon her.

In the west, as she crossed the threshold
and looked up at the sky, there glowed before
her eyes a windy trouble of sunset. The
almost leafless branches of the elms at the
foot of the garden showed black and sharp
against the angry red background, which had
something threatening in its sullen silence of
gathering clouds, blown hurriedly to and fro,
and anon uprearing themselves in wrestling
shapes of giants and uncouth beasts. A
sound of breeding winds was abroad. The
shrubberies whispered drearily in the deepening twilight; whilst the fallen yellow leaves,
" pale as remembrance in a shallow heart,"
stirred uneasily beneath the wintry breath of
the November evening. A solitary bat (lin-

gering yet a little ere he hung himself up in barn or belfry for his long sleep) flittered hither and thither among the shadows, the very ghost of the joyous winged life of song and sunbeam vanished with the summer.

Along the road towards the city, where the lights were already beginning to gleam, Margaret Oglevie walked steadily and quickly, her head slightly bowed, her prayer-book in her hand. The news about Richard Eliot had moved her strongly. It seemed to the girl's pure and pitying mind so sad a thing that a young life should thus drift away into the darkness, should thus be bruised and disfigured by contact with evil; and she felt an infinite compassion for the sinner, a great yearning to help him in his loneliness and peril.

"Oh, he *must* be so unhappy!" sighed Margaret; for she remembered in their many talks together how often he had revealed a love of things lovely, a natural capacity for high thought, a generous sympathy with noble action. And to think of him, out of reach of all better influences, with none to speak encouragement or consolation in his hour of struggle against despair and doubt— this was terrible, intolerable to her !

So, rapt in commiserating meditation, the girl pursued her way, a slight, grey-cloaked figure, almost unconscious of the shifting life that filled the narrow streets she passed through. Entering The Close, she beheld the tall spire of the Cathedral standing out clear and still against the wild sky, rising solemnly from among the shadows and brood- ing darkness of the lower world into the purer air above, and lifting the eye from earth heavenward. The deep voice of the organ was wandering round the walls, and surging upward to the roof of the Cathedral, as Margaret stole silently down the nave to

where the slender congregation was gathered.
Then the voice of the organ died away, and
the voice of the priest took up the accents
of prayer, and praise, and sorrowful confession.

". . . We have erred and strayed from
Thy ways like lost sheep. We have followed
too much the devices and desires of our own
hearts. We have offended against Thy holy
laws. We have left undone those things
which we ought to have done; and we
have done those things which we ought not
to have done; and there is no health in
us. . ."

Surely the prayers of loving and fervent-
hearted women are powerful to reach God,
and intercede for men! Who but must
recognise (whatsoever creed he hold) the
beauty and meetness of conception that makes
a woman our mediator at the Throne!

Margaret Oglevie prayed deeply and

earnestly for Richard Eliot (as, indeed, she would pray for all such of her friends as were in any sort afflicted or distressed) ; and when the service was ended, she rose up and went on her way quieted and comforted.

" Miss Oglevie !"

Margaret was passing beneath the upper archway leading from the precincts of The Close, when thus accosted. Turning her head, she beheld Oscar Dale.

" Mr. Dale! Oh, I'm so glad to have met you! I want to ask you about Richard Eliot. You'll tell me what you can, won't you ?"

" About Dick ? Of course I will, Miss Oglevie. Stupid fellow! I'm quite angry with him! Why couldn't he have more confidence in us all, instead of going off in such an insane fashion ? However, I suppose it'll be the usual fatted calf business at The

Leas before long—(what a shame, by-the-way, innocent animals should be thus sacrificed to man's misconduct! Not much joy over the sinner that repents, I should think, amongst young cattle !)—for of course he'll turn up as soon as he's had time for reflection."

"You believe he will ? I hope so, most sincerely! I liked him so much," said Margaret, simply. " Didn't you ?"

"Yes, confound him ! I *did*. Won't we just bully him when he comes back ! Why, I'd have settled the wretched seven hundred myself, if he had only let me know I could serve him ! It's too bad !"

" *Seven* hundred ? Mrs. Towle said it was eleven."

" Ah ! I like Mrs. Towle. I suppose, too, she favours that other charitable report— that charming cock-and-bull—or Goose and Gridiron—story about a female ' Boots,' or something of the sort ?"

"I *knew* it wasn't true," exclaimed Margaret, the tears springing to her eyes, and the colour coming to her cheek. "Oh, it's cruel, it's wicked, to credit such ill things, and to be so ready to spread them! I can't think how people *can!*"

"To err is human. To make the most of the error (if it's not one's own), is also human. There's something, I believe, connected with erring that's divine; but that doesn't concern Mrs. Towle. Divinity may hedge her husband (he's a parson, so I suppose it must), but it don't affect his wife. She's the wrong side the fence. . . . . By-the-bye, Miss Oglevie, you're not walking home alone, are you?"

"Well, no! I was to go to the Regent, and be called for by our man Dixon. He has been sent to the station to fetch a hamper, I think; and after that he is to drive me home."

"Just so. I—I rather wanted to see your father," said Mr. Dale, with a certain hesitation, somewhat new to him.

"Then come back with me in the dog-cart, will you not? Or should we walk?"

Mr. Dale pronounced strongly in favour of walking, and, having left a message at the hotel for Mr. Oglevie's servant, the two started for The Coppice. In Queen Street they passed Sophia Towle, who, with a friend, had been attending the Cathedral service.

"Well, I never!" cried Sophia. "*Did* you see that, Miss Bailey? Maggie Oglevie and Mr. Dale! It's dreadful, my dear, how she runs after him! Mamma says it's quite indelicate."

"And so it is!" said Miss Bailey. But then, unlike poor Margaret, both these young ladies had enjoyed the blessings of maternal teaching, which had sanctioned only expur-

gated Shaksperes, had held such a work as
" Adam Bede " " highly improper," and had
boggled at nude statuary. People of this
description are of the order of "*nice* persons,"
whom Swift defines as " persons of nasty
ideas," and are closely allied to that section
of the British public (no inconsiderable one)
whose literary enlightenment Ralph Oglevie
caustically summed up by saying that it
"strains at a Swinburne and swallows a
Tupper !"

Miss Towle was mistaken when she asserted
that Margaret Oglevie ran after Mr. Dale.
(She might as truly have asserted that
Atalanta " ran after " her suitors !) But had
she reversed the names there would, perhaps,
have been some sort of foundation for her
statement. Oscar Dale was unquestionably
attracted by Margaret. Since coming to
man's estate he had spent ten years in the
world, and had seen more phases of life than

one. He had known women all head, like Becky Sharp, and women all heart, like Amelia Sedley; but, until meeting Margaret, he had never known a woman combining the two in any noteworthy degree. Nor was it alone the gifts she already possessed which made men think well of her : there was the rich promise contained in these gifts. She was but nineteen, and her character had yet to develop itself, as the budding rose has to develop the folded fragrance and beauty that fill its heart.

"Were you at the Cathedral?" asked Margaret, as soon as they had fairly left the din of the streets behind them. "I didn't see you."

"But I saw you," said Dale. "I came early, and had been wandering about those ' serious avenues,' the cloisters."

"How quiet and beautiful they always are! Whenever I walk through them I think of the 'Pensive nun, devout and pure, sober, steadfast, and demure!' Did it ever strike you what a wonderful combination of adjectives that is? I was reading this morning, in my 'Autocrat,' something Holmes says about words that have loved one another from the cradle of the language, but have never been wedded until the poet brought them together."

"Do you often go to the Cathedral?" asked Dale, after a pause.

"Very often. It does me so much good when I am feeling tired or troubled. There's such a harmony between the place and the service; it soothes one more, I think, than anything else possibly could. '*This is the House of Fulfilment of Craving!*'—that's what I feel when I come into it, away from the streets. Then there's the organ!"

"Ah, the organ! What an instrument it is!—as majestic as Milton, as human as

Shakspere! Don't you know how Dick
Eliot used to 'go it' about the organ ?"

" I know he loved music," answered Margaret, thoughtfully. " Finish telling me
what you can of him at Oxford, will you ?
How does Mrs. Eliot take it ?"

" Very sensibly, I assure you. Indeed,
she seems less upset about the matter than
her husband. She says she supposes young
men *will* do these wild things ; and she told
me a story of Lord Somebody or other, when
a minor, which appeared to comfort her considerably."

" Mr. Dale, I shall not listen to you it
you intend being sarcastic. Well ? Please
go on !"

" As for Charles Eliot, he of course agrees
with me that Dick, on second thoughts, will
act like a sane person, and come home. But
if he doesn't turn up by the end of the week,
we propose inserting a notice to him in the

second column of the *Times*, telling him his difficulties are all settled, and so forth, and that we are only waiting his return to fat the kilted calf—I mean kill the fatted calf. It would really serve him right to have veal the first day he's back ; he does dislike it so !"

" Mr. Eliot has gone to Oxford, has he not ?"

" Yes ; he went the day before yesterday. I heard from him this morning, and things are really not so bad as one might suppose. Indeed, I think the authorities of St. Sepulchre's intend reconsidering their sentence ; and, in that case, they would naturally make it lighter."

" I'm sure I hope they will! Then, Richard Eliot——"

Here Margaret stopped herself abruptly. Mr. Dale continued, as though not noticing the fact.

" The total of it all is, Miss Oglevie, that

Dick has been foolish—nothing more! There certainly is some slight mystery about the disappearance of this Abingdon young person ; but then we, who know our friend, needn't trouble ourselves about that, I think. Coincidences are as common as blackberries nowadays—result of over population—and a fellow can't even make a fool of himself but some one goes and copies the process. Most discouraging to youthful enterprise, isn't it ?"

Margaret laughed ; and here the subject dropped, for they had reached The Coppice.

CHAPTER IV.

"THRO' DEPTH TO DEPTH MORE BLEAK AND SHADY."

FROM the sublime to the ridiculous is but a step—only that step is the goose-step. And as slight a distance divides other extremes (void, perhaps, of sublimity, although open to ridicule) of our mundane existence; so that the space between affluence and indigence, between honour and dishonour, pleasure and pain, is often traversed at a stride. And it is sad, it is terrible, to think with what fatal facility we who walk the earth, marching graveward, may make the one false or foolish move that alters the current of our days.

> " Alas ! how easily things go wrong—
> A sigh too much, or a kiss too long ;
> And there follows a mist and a weeping rain,
> And life is never the same again !"

Let us take a look at our hero, six weeks
after the hour when, like young Lochinvar,
he came out of the west, leaving Oxford and
seeking London. It is ten o'clock in the
morning of a mid-December day. The scene
is a small bed-room on the second-floor back
of a house in the near neighbourhood of the
Angel, Islington—a house which the rolling
thunder of traffic from the great main
thoroughfare causes to rattle its window-
frames, and, figuratively, to shake in its shoes.
The occupants of the bedroom are two—a
man and a dog ; Richard Eliot, and his
terrier, Satan. The former is just finishing
dressing, the latter is critically watching the
process. On the top of the low chest of
drawers which serves as toilet-table, and
placed beside the small looking-glass (an

article perversely given to turning somer-
saults, presenting its wooden back to one when
most its face is in request), are a tumbler
of water, a penny roll, and a bottle of benzine.
The two first-named constitute Dick's breakfast (the bread having been purchased over-
night, and brought home wrapped in a remnant of *Lloyd's Weekly;*) whilst the benzine
is intended to correct a certain incipient seedi-
ness that has lately betrayed itself about
Dick's outer garments.

Dick eats his roll (which he shares with
his dog), washes it down with a draught of
water, and then, throwing his coat across his
knee (where it lies with dangling arms, like a
limp boy about to be whipped), and taking a
piece of rag in his hands, he proceeds to his
task of renovation. Perhaps some thought
of the days, not yet distant, when he was
more apt to besprinkle himself with Eau-de-
Cologne than with this less-favoured scent,

may have arisen in his mind, since a rather
rueful expression comes over his face—a face
paler, graver, and with a perceptibly older
look about it than when we saw it last.
For the past six weeks have told upon him
in many ways.

Reaching London, our ex-Oxonian had
taken a first night's shelter at an hotel hard
by the terminus he arrived at. Next day,
when the warmth and excitement of mo-
mentous action had evaporated, and he found
himself fairly committed to the friendless,
unfathomed sea of dubious adventure, he was
conscious of a certain chill at heart, a certain
re-awakened appreciation of the shore he had
forsaken. His inner vision persistently wandered backward, and, like Orpheus of old,
or Lot's retrospective wife, he turned eloquent
eyes after the glory departed.

But a course of conduct had to be deter-
mined on, and the first thing to do was to

form an estimate of his material resources. These, upon examination, were found to consist of seven shillings in silver, threepence-halfpenny in copper, a watch in gold, an overcoat, and a portmanteau, whose hurried packing had brought together the following articles :—Four shirts, three socks (a pair and an odd one), six collars, a handkerchief, a wristband, a clothesbrush, a comb, a writing-case, a carte-de-visite album, a photograph (framed) of The Leas, a dozen volumes of poetry and romance, a packet of letters (tied with a bootlace), and a vast quantity of manuscript. This last item, indeed, was the most considerable of all, and was regarded by Dick with the fondness of a parent for a good-for-nothing child, to whose manifold failings the paternal eyes are blind.

With these possessions in hand, Dick prepared to begin life on his own account. His ready money discharged his bill at the hotel ;

whilst, by pledging his watch, he raised a further sum of three pounds, for future emergencies. He then set forth in quest of a lodging, which, after divers discomforting encounters with mercenary females (whereby his utter incapacity to deal with the London landlady was promptly made manifest), he discovered at No. 33, Paradise Terrace, New Jerusalem Street, Islington. Here he secured a bedroom (" with the use of sitting-room ") at a weekly rental of seven shillings, payable in advance — gas, coals, and boot-cleaning extra.

A month Dick passed uneventfully beneath this roof, taking his meals promiscuously in small eating-houses and coffee-shops, and spending monotonous hours in dingy newsrooms, reading or writing. In these latter resorts (Deacon's, in Leadenhall Street, was one ; Peele's, at the corner of Fetter Lane, another ; a place adjoining the Charing Cross

Theatre, a third) he would copy out his precious effusions with infinite patience and care, tenderly heedful of comma and colon, and keenly alive to the crossing of t's or dotting of i's. Then, having read and re-read them over to himself in semi-audible tones, he would hopefully despatch them to the editors of such periodicals as the " Cornhill," " Temple Bar," " Blackwood's," "All the Year Round," and the like, accompanied by elaborately modest notes, and enclosing stamps in case of rejection. Thus sanguinely did Dick cast his bread upon the waters, and after many days it returned unto him ; for the editors one and all agreed in declining his contributions—and when the editors do agree, their unanimity is wonderful. Poor Dick had secretly relied on his manuscripts as weapons wherewith he should conquer fortune ; but, if they were weapons at all, they were weapons like the boomerang, coming back to their projector as fast as they were sent forth. It was disheartening.

Finding his literary efforts thus unappreciated, Dick reluctantly turned his attention toward other possibilities of existence. " X. Y. Z." (said the *Times*) required a gentleman of good education and ability as private secretary. Dick offered himself to " X. Y. Z.," but " X. Y. Z." would none of him. " Bona Fides " sought the same, waiving, however, the education, and only insisting on ability in so far as went the ability to deposit three hundred pounds cash, for which the amplest security was awaiting. " Veritas " wanted a steady, well-conducted clerk for his counting-house ; but, alas ! with all his steadiness and good conduct, "Veritas" didn't want our hero. Jones needed a night-porter, and Brown demanded a single-handed waiter ; but neither Jones nor Brown would accept the services of Richard Eliot as his assistant. And so with other advertisers.

Meanwhile, as the weeks went by, and Mrs.
McNab, his landlady, became urgent and un-
pleasant respecting his arrears of rent, way-
laying her lodger on the stairs as he left the
house at morning or returned at night.   O
ye gods ! the horror and torture of being at
the mercy of a coarse, shrewish woman, whose
every word grates upon the nerves and turns
one's heart sick with humiliation.   Let us
be Tantalus, Sisyphus, Sindbad the Sailor,
with the Old Men of the Sea *ad lib.*—let us
be Caliban with his cramps, Enceladus under
Ætna, Prometheus on Caucasus, any one, anything !—but save us, Heaven, from owing a
penny to the professional letter of lodgings !
Dick Eliot used to come home like a thief in
the night, stealing up the stairs on tiptoe for
fear of evoking the harpy McNab from the
lair she called her "settin'-room."   Sometimes
he would pace up and down the pavement
opposite the house, waiting until all its lights

were extinguished, when he would venture
to let himself in, and wearily hide his di-
minished head beneath the bedclothes. "And
this," groaned the poor fellow with bitterest
humour, " this is merry Islington !"

One dripping December night (it was the
fifteenth of the month), on trying the door
with his latchkey, he found it fastened against
him. After some hesitation, he gave a faint
apologetic pull at the bell, and at the end of
ten minutes, no notice being taken of his
appeal, he hazarded a second. This was
equally unsuccessful; and so with a third and
fourth. Then the truth became evident to
him. Mrs. McNab had taken the law into
her own hands, had locked her lodger out, and
confiscated his goods and chattels.

" So be it," muttered Dick turning slowly
away from the door; " I suppose I must
accept my ejectment. Come along, Satan,
old boy ! I've still a shilling left, and

that, at least, will get us a bed for to-night."

Our hero and his dog accordingly sought shelter in a small sixth-rate coffee-house; and in the morning, being penniless, Dick decided to pawn his overcoat.

Now, to deposit a watch, a chain, a diamond ring, or any similar valuable, in the hands of a respectable tradesman for the, temporary loan of a few pounds, is one thing; but to subside into the slums and haggle over the coat from off your back, is another. A dozen different pawnshops in and about the reeking, foul-breathed purlieus of Drury Lane did Dick Eliot pass and repass, without finding courage to enter one. Through the network of filth and misery, amid oyster-stalls and coster-mongers' barrows, and organ-grinders and orange-women; past fried-fish shops and eel-pie houses; by coal and potato-sheds and scrappy little butcheries; tumbling over crawl-

ing, half-clad children, and jostling against
drunken men and shrieking women; through
all the staring vice and poverty that breed
and fester in the narrow thoroughfares between St. Giles's and the Strand, Eliot of
Sepulchre's irresolutely made his way, and
eventually screwed himself up to carry out
the intention that had brought him into the
unwholesome neighbourhood.

In a little closet-like aperture (one of a row
of half-a-dozen), looking over a greasy counter
into the shop proper, our hero hurriedly explained the nature of his business. The
pawnbroker's assistant made a keen, critical
examination of the proffered garment, letting
fall a series of disparaging remarks concerning
its cut and condition as he did so—remarks
which caused its owner to grow hot with
shame and anger.

" What d'ye want on it ?" quoth the critic.

" A sovereign," said Dick.

" A sovereign ! Why, we'd sell *you* a better harticle at seventeen-and-six. Say hate shillin', and you'll be nigher the figger."

" Yes, very well ; that'll do."

The man rolled up the coat into a bundle with marvellous quickness, pinned a ticket to it, and threw it into the darkness behind him, where Dick could faintly discern dusky bales, and piles of wearing apparel, and dingy gowns hanging from the ceiling like the head- less wives of Bluebeard. So soon as he had received his eight shillings (less the sum of one halfpenny, deducted for the ticket), he hastened to escape the neighbourhood, taking a turn or two amid the fruits and flowers of Covent Garden to purify him of its evil odours.

Thence he adjourned to the luncheon-bar of a public-house at the corner of Garrick Street, where he obtained a plate of cold meat and a glass of beer. This disposed of,

he took his way to a Leicester Square news-
room, and waded wearily through the papers,
in the hope of discovering a means of meeting
or escaping his present necessities. Nothing
of the kind, however, revealed itself; so Dick
paid his penny, and sallied forth into the
streets once again, securing, ere nightfall, a
week's lodging for the sum of four shillings
and sixpence.

He had been attracted to this economical
refuge by an advertisement in the *Telegraph,*
couched as follows :

" Respectable Lodgings for Single Gentlemen, at 4s. 6d. per week. All separate
sleeping compartments. Use of sitting-room,
daily papers, and library.—Address, Alexsandringham Chambers, 87, Job Street,
Oxford Street, W."

This was a curious place, and it was a
curious life that the single gentlemen who
inhabited it were accustomed to lead. All

day long, in a dingy, tobacco-clouded room, over an undertaker's shop, they sat in a semicircle around the fire, puffing their pipes in silence, like a drowsy council of Indian chiefs. A dense haze of smoke was ever hovering above their heads (typical of the social cloud under which each and all of the single gentlemen confessedly were), and occasionally a pot of beer was passed' languidly from one to the other. Faded failures of men were most of them—men with a used, second-hand look about them, and yet with a Micawberish confidence in the future that lent eloquence to their words whenever they awoke into conversation. This faith, however, was altogether passive, and evoked no accompanying energy of action. Exertion, indeed, seemed as far from their thoughts as it was with Tennyson's thin-voiced lotus-eaters. They seldom stirred out into the open air; but they were greatly given to writing letters. They didn't appear to eat ; they only smoked. Sometimes two would withdraw themselves from the circle and play monotonous games of cribbage, making marking-pegs of lucifer-matches, and moistening dirty thumbs with dull-hued lips to deal and separate the sticky, cornerless cards. They read the *Times* and *Telegraph,* supplied them at morning, and the *Standard,* which came to them at evening, from beginning to end, tearing them up into pipe-lights on the succeeding day. They went to the old worm-eaten bookcase in the corner of the room, and dragged forth dusty, dilapidated volumes with missing middles and incomplete endings. This was the library. Odd numbers of the " Penny Encyclopædia," Guides to Bath and its Neighbourhood, Catalogues of the Great Exhibition of '51, Mining Prospectuses, Addresses delivered on various forgotten occasions, and Sermons of unknown

divines — these formed the staple of the
literature of which the single gentlemen (*vide*
advertisement) had the use.

As for the bedrooms, they were merely
little cells, or loose boxes, ranged on either
side a long, white-washed, sky-lighted corridor, and so far separated as a wooden
partition some seven feet high could effect
the object. By standing on one's scanty
straw-stuffed bed, one could overlook one's
neighbours, both to right and left; but, as
each room was a duplicate of one's own, and
each tenant a smoke-dried copy of his fellows,
the temptation to do so was not a strong
one.

For the rest, a small wash-house at the end
of the corridor, furnished with a water-tap, a
stone sink, and tin basins, completed the
attractions of Alexsandringham Chambers.

In this atmosphere of mental and moral
Rip Van Winkleism, by dint of a further

pawning of waistcoat, collar, and necktie, our hero contrived to subsist for a matter of eight days, paying an extra shilling for the extra night he remained beyond the week's end. At the expiration of this term he found himself thrown upon the streets, semi-clad and penniless, just as the comfortless old age of the year was drawing to its close, and the bells of Yule were ringing forth the declaration of peace on earth, goodwill to men.

CHAPTER V.

DICK'S CHRISTMAS.

A GOOD many people, doubtless, have known what it is to be houseless and homeless, without bed or bread; but not of these, we imagine, is the general novel-reader. More likely will such sorry experience have been that of the novel-*writer*; for where we hear of the hardships of one Murger, Villon, Poe, or Savage, there are a hundred lesser men of letters—mute, inglorious Miltons—who have suffered and made no sign. The path of literature is a very *viâ dolorosa*, abounding in thorns and stony places, and sloughs of despond. A few, through luck or wit, or "by reason of strength," may attain the heights made golden with the sun of success; but a host of others faint and fall by the wayside, and "die with all their music in them." They are weighed down with the burden of contributions declined, and they carry a pack, like that of Christian, heavy with rejected MSS.—sins which have returned unto their parents. And it is well if they bear it in the Christian spirit.

When Richard Eliot found himself wholly *in extremis,* "with nothing but the sky for a great-coat," and without place to lay his head, or food to fill his stomach, it may reasonably be wondered that he did not cast pride to the winds, and hie home to that feast of fatted calf whereof Mr. Dale had made prophecy; even though he should have to eat humble-pie as a first course. But, mobile and yielding as was our hero in many respects, he had at bottom a stubborn spirit of resolve which, once aroused, was not readily overcome. The feeling may have been a morbid one, the shame a false shame; but, even when starvation stared him in the face, he could not bring himself to turn back upon the road he had chosen. Not that he was impenitent, or hard of heart—quite the reverse. He was willing enough to own the error of· his ways, to admit his folly to the full; but he shrank from acknowledging—as tacitly he would, did he play out the prodigal to the sequel—that he quailed before the consequences of the step he had taken. His hardihood was that of the soldier, with whom it requires more daring to run away than to remain in the ranks. Aunt Deborah had always denounced him as "lamentably deficient in moral courage" (a quality which with her meant not simply indifference to the feelings of others, but an alacrity in showing it), and something of the sort, we suppose, was what ailed him.

It was Christmas Eve when Dick first entered upon his term of unqualified vagrancy, of vagabondage pure and simple. In the course of the day the proprietor of the Alexsandringham Chambers had made a round of rent-collecting among the more dubiously solvent of his tenants, and, on Dick admitting his inability to pay for another night's lodging, he had briefly, but emphatically, announced him the alternative.

" Parties," he explained, " who came without luggage couldn't remain without money; it stood to reason."

Dick said, " Is that it?" rather absently ; and, on the landlord assuring him that that was it, he replied, " Oh ! all right," and walked out of the place.

It is a queer sensation, that of houselessness in a great city—of being homeless among a thousand homes. To feel that it matters nothing whether you turn your steps east, west, north, or south; that, whichever way you go, you are as far from a haven at the end of the day as at the beginning—this is dispiriting, bewildering! Coming suddenly into the purposeful din and movement of Oxford Street, Dick hesitated forlornly; then, with a short laugh of impatience and contempt at his needless vacillation, he took his way westward. It was between two and three of the afternoon. A gleam of watery sunlight had broken through the cloud-roof of doleful grey overhead, glancing here and there on the shining panels and silver-plated harness of brougham or carriage, as it drew up before one or other of the long line of gaily-decked shops, setting down stately women in costly furs and rustling silks. For the world of wealth and fashion was abroad at this hour, busy buying Christmas presents and decora-

tions; and an air of festive preparation seemed
to pervade the entire district. Instinctively
beginning his walk as though with some
definite end in view, Dick turned to the left
on reaching the Circus, and proceeded down
Regent Street. Here, in the brief sunlight,
the stream of fashionable life, sparkling and
shallow, flowed gaily enough along its broad
granite-bedded channel. The shop-windows
were tricked out with their brightest and
best; all the wonderful, bewitching wares of
Vanity Fair lay open to London eyes. Mr.
Sala—the Wandering Jew of journalists—has
called Regent Street an avenue of superfluities.
And so, indeed, it is. Knick-knacks, gim-
cracks, gewgaws, kickshaws, fal-lals, and
frippery. " And all the rest " (as Mr. Pope
of Twick'nham hath it) " is leather and
prunella !"

Unregarded amidst the brilliant throng
of daintily attired women and happy, eager-

eyed children—of superb young dandies (the
listless lords of too much leisure) and
their carefully preserved seniors—of majestic
flunkeys, that "blushed with crimson and
blazed with gold"—Dick moved aimlessly
onward, too wholly preoccupied with his own
dreary thoughts to take heed of the society
about him. Nevertheless, the sharp contrast
between all this ease and affluence and luxury
and his lonely destitution was darkly present
in his mind, albeit he shrank from the bitterness of a full realisation of the position. But
presently, by an accident, this was forced
upon him. A fair, proud-lipped young beauty,
passing from her carriage to a jeweller's shop,
came into momentary contact with him as
their paths crossed. Instinctively she drew
back and swept aside her dress from his
touch, with a gesture of disdain, her imperious
eyes glancing at his shabby figure, at his
frayed and worn coat, tightly buttoned to

hide the absence of waistcoat and collar, as
she did so. The lost colour flamed back into
Dick's pale face, as though he had been
struck. Uncovering,• he hastily stood by,
bareheaded, to let her pass before him, a
mingling of apology and protest in his
attitude. The girl was of gentle blood and
breeding, and slightly bowed her head in
acknowledgment, as she took precedence.
Then the crowd closed up after her, and Dick
went on with the tide.

But the incident had aroused him to an
acute sense of the realities of his situation.
Coming to a window wherein was displayed
a full-length pier-glass, he paused to survey
himself. Truly, his appearance was a sorry
one! His coat was unquestionably shabby;
his hat looked seedy (rain had played the
mischief with both); his boots were un-
polished. Putting a hand in his pocket, he
felt for his last penny. He was hungry and

thirsty; he had tasted nothing since the night before, and he could not say where another meal would come from; but, nevertheless, in neither bread nor beer should this, his sole remaining coin, be expended! Dick went and got his boots cleaned.

The action was characteristic; akin to that of a Foolish Virgin who should use her last drop of oil not to feed her lamp, but to brighten her tresses withal. There was about it a certain audacity, a certain courageous extravagance which had its root in something deeper, worthier, than mere vanity. In such spirit have men arrayed themselves in their gayest to mount the steps of the scaffold; and thus did Sardanapalus clothe himself in royal robes that he might meet his fate right royally.

Soon the carriages and their owners began to lessen in number and turn homeward. For a while the roll of wheels westward was continuous, like the sound of a spring tide, subdued by distance, upon a shingly beach. Anon a million jets of gas, within and without the shops, leapt into life, and flickering leagues of lights marked out the course of the teeming streets. Unheedful whither he went, Dick had wandered through Leicester Square, and past the National Gallery to Charing Cross. Here he entered the station, now, on Christmas Eve, tenfold busier than ever. Signs of the season were on all sides —in the crowds of holiday-makers, hurrying and hurried off in densely packed trains to the firesides of kith and kin ; in the bunches of holly and mistletoe they carried ; in the glad Christmas greetings and good wishes they exchanged ; in the piled-up hampers of game, cases of wine, and barrels of oysters which the porters and their trucks were overwhelmed with. Dick sat him down upon a bench, and watched the bewildering scene,

himself apparently the one creature without
aim or interest—expecting nothing, expected
by none, of all the shifting thousands about
him.

His thoughts were heavy and bitter, his
face sadder than slate roof beneath an
autumn drizzle.   At home at The Leas now,
he mused, the log-fed fires are burning
brightly ; the shutters are closed,' the windows curtained ; the dinner-table is glisten-
ing with glass and silver; warmth and
light and comfort are everywhere.   He
fancied his father seated beside the glowing hearth, the dear old dogs, Kelpie and
Sir Walter, water-spaniel and deer-hound,
stretched on the rug at his feet.   He saw
his comely mother moving about the room,
putting little feminine finishing touches to the
arrangement of the table, adding this or
altering that.   Perhaps Oscar Dale was with
them (they were wont to have friends on

Christmas Eve) ; perhaps Mr. Oglevie and Margaret.

Would they think, were they thinking of him ? · Ah ! if they but saw him now ! with what tender forgiveness and compassion would they not welcome him to their midst ! Should he rise up and go to them ? He had been wild and wicked, foolish and perverse ; but he knew they would pardon all. But then how should he stand in his own eyes, did he thus return ? Would he not seem weak and cowardly, faint of heart and infirm of purpose ? Besides—it was too late to think of this ; the time for drawing back had gone by. A hundred long miles lay between him and home, and, even with the will, he had neither the power to reach it nor the means of communication. Too late, too late !

How long Dick Eliot remained seated within the station he did not know ; but

eventually he was aroused from his re-
verie by a touch on the shoulder from an
inspector. Was he going off anywhere by
train? No. What was he doing there,
then? Nothing. In that case, said the
official, with seasonable jocularity, he'd better
go and do nothing in some other place, where
there was more room and less need of it;
they couldn't have loafers about the platform
on Christmas Eve.

Dick made no answer, but mutely got up
and went forth into the streets again. Cold,
and damp, and hunger had begun to make
him submissive. He walked towards Westminster, passed by the shadows of the Abbey,
and came to the Bridge. He leant wearily
over the parapet, and watched the dark flow
of water underneath, and listened to the
monotonous lapping of the tide against the
sodden wooden piers and slippery stonework
below him. East and west the riverside

lights of London cast blurred and wavering
reflections deep into the passing stream—
reflections weirdly lengthening and contracting, that writhed, snake-like, and flashed,
and broke, and quiveringly re-appeared.
Ghostly barges, black and funereal as craft
of Charon, slid through the shadow-haunted
arches, and vanished into the darkness as
silently. Now and again a hoarse cry, as of
warning, was borne up from the nether gloom,
only to die away forlornly, and leave all still,
save for the persistent wash and whisper of
the river against its banks.

Leaving Westminster Bridge, Dick retraced
his steps to the Strand. Going down this, he
passed under Temple Bar, through Fleet
Street, up Farringdon Street, and so round
by Holborn into Oxford Street again. But
he was unconscious of the direction he took,
and ignorant, for the most part, of the names
of the thoroughfares he traversed. He suf-

fered chance to guide his feet, loitering here,
and halting there, on the lightest pretext
for relieving the dreary tedium of his pil-
grimage.

At length, after long hours, the stream of
life with which he drifted began visibly to
slacken and subside.   First the larger shops
closed, then the lesser.   Oyster and supper-
rooms, small confectioners, tobacconists, and
the like, lingered to the last, keeping the
crowded public-houses company until midnight
and one o'clock.   Then these, too, turned out
their lamps and their drunkards, and fitfully
and uneasily the wide city began to sink into
slumber.   The last cab rattled by, the last
tipsy brawler reeled out of hearing.   Presently, with a snatch of ribald song upon
their painted lips, three women brushed by
Dick as he stood aside in the partial shadow
of a doorway.

"Hullo, you !" cried one, catching sight of

him. "Come and stand us a drink, there's a beauty! It's Christmas time, you know, and we don't meet every night. Won't you?"

The other two looked at him, and passed on; but the one who had spoken lingered behind.

"You ain't offended, are you? I s'pose you're off home?"

"*Home!* . . . I have none."

There was that in Dick's voice which caused the girl to draw nearer and change her tone.

"No home? Honour bright? Let's look at you!"

She placed her hand on his shoulder and turned his face toward her. Then, with some sudden impulse, she lightly lifted his hat and put back the hair from his forehead with a touch wholly womanly and pitiful.

"Lizzie, you fool! come along, can't you?" shouted back one of her companions, angrily;

and, without speaking further, the girl hurried off.

Somehow, the tears had found their way to Dick Eliot's eyes, as he looked after her.

*   *   *   *   *

Charles Dickens, in one of his later sketches, tells us how, when the last sparks of London night-life have disappeared, the yearning of the houseless mind is for any sign of company. any lighted place, any movement, anything suggestive of any one being up—or even so much as awake ; for the houseless eye looks out for lights in windows.

Thus it was with our hero. Hours passed; overhead the church clocks chimed *two, three, four,* in the dull air ; and still he stole miserably through the rainy, gusty streets (deserted of all save an occasional policeman and " persons rascal and forlorn," outcasts like himself), the horror of solitude weighing ever more heavily upon him. But for the presence of his dog Satan, who, wet and weary as his master, had followed him dumbly in all his wanderings, he would have given way wholly to despair.

At four o'clock, on an ordinary morning, would come the first symptoms of returning day-life and labour. Early workmen, with long distances to go to their tasks, would begin to appear in the streets, stopping at small coffee-stalls to take breakfast—steaming pints of coffee and inch-thick slices of bread-and-butter. Cabs, with drowsy fares from the hotels, would splash by on their way to catch the first trains from town. Market wagons, piled with cabbages, would rumble and stagger over the stones toward Covent Garden. (These are the advance-guard of the vast army that has soon to begin another day's march.) The public-houses—latest to bed and earliest to rise—would once more light their lamps; and gradually, and almost imperceptibly, the city awakes—the streets fill.

But this morning, being Christmas, it was otherwise. The work-a-day world lingered luxuriously over its repose, grateful for the unwonted liberty to rest from toil and turmoil. And thus it befell that Dick's long, unhappy watches of the night were made hours longer than would have been the case but for the holiday ; nor was it until there came the quiet, quick-footed man to turn out the gas-lamps, and the grey-bedraggled dawn struggled tearfully into undisputed existence, that his forlorn solitude began to be relieved.

Throughout the day—Christmas Day— Dick Eliot, faint and footsore, tramped the interminable streets, with their endless alien faces and unheeding thousands. Late in the afternoon, he crept into St. Paul's, smuggling his dog in with him beneath his coat. Service was going on ; but he sought out a

distant recess in the wall, aloof from the congregation, and stretching himself on the stone
seat it contained, fell at once into a heavy,
troubled slumber. When he awoke the service was over, the people leaving. With the
crowd he went also ; and now the night had
again to be encountered.

This was passed much as was its predeces-
sor, save that exhaustion made him less alive
to its misery. From time to time he would
seek shelter beneath an occasional porch, or
sink down on some bare, rain-beaten doorstep,
snatching a wretched dog-sleep for a brief
half-hour, and waking with a start, as if from
nightmare, cramped and chilled to the bone.

Shall we linger over his sufferings ? We,
who have undergone the same distress, have
felt the same despair, and had the devil
tempting us with the same idea of ending it
all—we could continue the picture and fill in
its pitiful details to the last touch. But to

what good ?   For whose pleasure—our own
or our reader's ?   Bah !   The reading can
scarcely be more cheerful than the recollection.
Let us lift the veil a little.

For two days and two nights Dick Eliot
had eaten nothing; and now, on the third
morning, a strange apathy and torpor seemed
to come over him.   The pangs of hunger he
no longer felt, and the sight of food in the
shop windows was even distasteful to him.
Without knowing whither he went, with a
vague swimming before his eyes, a dull, con-
fused humming in his ears, he took his way
through Trafalgar Square into St. James's
Park, where, drowsy with exhaustion, he sat
himself down on a bench in The Mall.

Some ten minutes later a pale, poorly-
dressed young fellow came and took possession
of the unoccupied end of the same seat, just
glancing at Dick's half-reclining figure as he
did so.

" That's a nice little dog you have there," said the stranger, after a pause, in a clear, kindly voice.

Dick was resting his head against the tree by which the bench was placed, and made no response either by word or motion.

" A capital little dog !" continued the speaker, undismayed by the apparent coolness of his reception. " Will he beg ? I once had a dog that would beg ten minutes at a time. ' Magnum Bonum,' I used to say (his name was Magnum Bonum) ' Magnum Bonum, old boy, beg !' And then the beggar would beg away as hard as he could for—well, for certainly *eight* minutes. What do you call your dog ? Eh ! what—why, good heavens ! the poor fellow's fainted !"

In a little time our hero came to himself again, and, on opening his eyes, perceived a gentle, womanly face bending over him, the while a soft voice sounded dreamily in his ears.

" Come, that's better, isn't it ? Oh, you'll
be as right as can be in a minute or two !
It's the heat, you know ! P—ff ! it *is* hot !
Sultriest December I ever knew.   Lean on
me as much as you like ; the more you lean
on me the better. *That's* the style ! Now,
as soon as you think you could manage to
walk a little, I'll help you home, you know."

" *Home !*" repeated Dick, bitterly—(everybody spoke to him of home !)—and he clenched
his hand with a gesture of despair.

" No, no ! of course not, of course not !
Too far off, as you say. My place is much
the nearer—much ! Just in Soho, you know;
Upper Storey Street. Take hold of my arm ;
don't be afraid ! There ! We shall get
along famously so. Now then !"

The two shabby young men (the one cling-
ing to the other, as a drowning person might
catch at a straw) moved slowly away toward
the steps of the Duke of York's Column ;

whilst Mr. Skillygolee (*alias* the Nasty Novice—late of the Penitentiary, Oak-cum-Pickering), emerging from behind an adjacent tree, adroitly whipped up the little terrier, Satan, and, muffling all remonstrance beneath a dirty fustian jacket, slipped stealthily off in the opposite direction.

CHAPTER VI.

WITH FRIENDS AT "THE LEAS."

ON the afternoon of the same day as that with which our last chapter closed, Charles Eliot was telling a story to the five little Draycotts—a Christmas story to a Christmas party. It was an annual affair, this gathering of his small kinsfolk at The Leas, and usually took place (as now) upon Boxing Day.

There had been an early one o'clock dinner for their special behoof, and as soon as it was over they had adjourned to the drawing-room.

Here they had seated themselves round the blazing fire, Baby Draycott (she was still

called Baby, although fully four years old)
being enthroned on Margaret Oglevie's lap,
from which post of 'vantage the robin-eyed
maiden could confront, with womanly forti-
tude, whatsoever evil magicians, ogres, ghosts,
or goblins Mr. Eliot's wondrous powers might
evoke from Bogieland.   Mrs. Eliot was lying
down in her bedroom, to sleep off a headache ; and thus Margaret Oglevie, who was
spending the day at The Leas, occupied the
place of hostess to the children.

Of these, Tom Draycott couched with Sir
Walter, the deerhound, on the hearthrug ;
Dora and Ethel shared the other dog, Kelpie,
between them, taking turns which should
have the head end ; whilst little Sydney had
stolen close to the story-teller's knee, whereon
he now trustfully rested a pair of small brown
hands, looking up to his face with wide eyes
of interest.

And this is how Charles Eliot began.

"Of course, you children all know that queer little insect, with a ribbed back and a score of legs, we call an 'old sow'—the creature that's something like a dark armadillo seen through the wrong end of a long telescope? Well, I once was acquainted with one. He was a bit of a musician, *my* friend was; and his favourite song used to be, '*When this Old Sow was New!*' an etymological version of '*When this Old Hat was New!*' He got at it thus:

1. When this old hat was new.
2. When this old sou'wester was new.
3. When this old sow was new.

Which was rather clever of him, wasn't it? And on Sundays, you know, instead of singing the Old Hundredth, as Nurse Dixon does, he'd sing the Old Sowsandth; and that's just ten times as good!"

Mr. Eliot!" exclaimed Margaret, laughing in spite of herself, "you're really *too* outrageous !"

"Oh please, *please* don't stop him, Miss Oglevie !" cried the children in chorus. "Tell on, Mr. Eliot !"

"Not if I'm subject to frivolous interruption," said Charles Eliot, eying Margaret Oglevie with affected severity ; whereat simple, warm-hearted little Ethel glanced quickly from one to the other with troubled eyes, and then stole her hand softly into Margaret's, against whom she was sitting.

"Never mind, Mr. Eliot," chorussed the children ; "she didn't mean ! Please tell on !"

So Mr. Eliot resumed.

"Where I first met my Old Sow was one day last summer in the hall, directly under the weather-glass. And I heard him say to it, 'Set fair, whatever you do !' just as Mrs. Gamp told Betsey Prig to drink fair, what-

ever she did.   For you must know that this
Old Sow was about starting off on a long, long
journey—in fact, he meant nothing less than
seeing the world and seeking his fortune.
First he was going to Norwich.   Then to the
North Pole ; then to the South.   Then to
the Eastern Hemisphere; then to the Western.
Then down the North Sea, or German Ocean,
through the Tropic of Capricorn, and so round
by the back way to Greenland's icy mountains.
And, last of all, he was going quietly across
the four quarters of the Globe—Europe,
Abram, Isaac, and America."

At this direful confusion of names there
rose a simultaneous outcry from Dora and
Tom ; Baby Draycott clapped her hands, and
the excitable Kelpie, breaking loose from
Ethel, dashed wildly round the room, barking
insanely.   When order was once more restored,
Mr. Eliot continued his story ; and now came
the interesting part.

For, repressing his inclination to simply
humorous extravagance, and having in view
the childrens' appreciation solely, he proceeded
to narrate, with delightful redundance of
detail, the thoroughly thrilling adventures of
his etymological hero in quest of his fortune,
bringing him into personal contact with all
the traditional glories of Fairyland — from
giants, and dwarfs, and lovely princesses, to
winged horses, wishing-caps, and enchanted
castles ; not to mention the King of the
Cannibal Islands, who was generously thrown
into the bargain. Just at the close of the
recital, when, lo and behold ! the Old Sow
turns into a Young Prince, " like Paris hand-
· some, and like Hector brave," there appeared
at the doorway Mr. Oscar Dale, in the nick
of time to share in the general satisfaction at
the happy ending of the story.

" It's like a tale Dick told us last summer
coming back from Idlewild," remarked Tom

Draycott. "Don't you remember, Dolly? Only Dick's had jollier fighting in it."

"And a witch and a black cat," added Dora, in a breath; "and a harp that played all by itself; and oh! how I wish Dick would come home again! Why *doesn't* Dick come home again?"

"Auntie Jane says Cousin Dick's been a naughty boy," observed little Sydney, solemnly.

"That I'm sure he hasn't!" burst out Ethel. "Dick's a very nice boy. Isn't Dick a nice boy, Miss Oglevie? I like Dick!"

"We all like Dick," said Margaret, gently. "But suppose you children run out in the garden for half-an-hour? It's quite light yet; and then, when you come in, you'll be ready for some tea."

"Aye! away with you!" cried Mr. Eliot; "and a chopper to chop off the last man's head!"

As the door closed after the children, the
smile with which Mr. Eliot had dismissed
them faded from his face, and he leant back
in his chair with a sigh, whereat the grey
old deerhound looked up at his master
with earnest eyes, and wagged a sympathetic
tail.

There was silence in the room for a minute
or two, during which the three persons at the
fireside gazed intently into the glowing depths
before them, conscious that each was thinking
on the same subject.   Charles Eliot was the
first to speak.

"Dale," he said, quietly, "I'm breaking
my heart about that boy of mine."

Oscar Dale, unlike Sir Walter, had no tail
wherewith to express sympathy, so he absently
laid hold of the poker, and thoughtfully poised
it in his hand.   Nor did Margaret Oglevie
either make any audible response.   Feeling
strongly, they said nothing.   The silence of

women and worldlings is often their most
exquisite eloquence.

"His mother, too, is fretting about him.
Alicia, as you know, is not one to give way
lightly ; but I can see that this prolonged
lack of even the slightest intelligence is telling on her sadly. If it were not for Miss
Oglevie here, I think she would quite lose
heart. But Margaret has been as good as
gold to us!" (Here Charles Eliot raised his
head, and spoke out with a certain fervent ring
in his voice that forcibly reminded one, at
least, of his companions of his absent son.)
"Yes, you have, Margaret! No girl could
have been more sweet and sensible. God
bless you for it!"

Oscar Dale, still balancing the poker in his
hand—for Englishmen, when at all moved,
instinctively grasp hold of something; their
hats, or the backs of chairs, or whatever may
be most available—glanced at Margaret whilst

Mr. Eliot was speaking. He saw her cheek pale a little, and her fingers busy themselves with a fold in her dress; but when she looked up to answer, there was a smile upon her lips, although tears glistened in her eyes.

"You make too much, Mr. Eliot, of the little I've been able to do for my friends' sake. Mrs. Eliot, you know, has been kind to me for years; and so have you! I should be a very sorry sort of creature if I didn't feel gratitude, and try to prove it—shouldn't I, Mr. Dale?"

"Ah, but I don't think you are one of the sorry sort, Miss Oglevie," said Oscar Dale, tapping a huge lump of coal emphatically with the poker. (So much he said, and no more; but the unspoken words which rose from his heart, and almost· expressed themselves in his voice, were "By Heaven! you're an angel! So gentle and loyal, so modest, and true, and tender. I swear I could fall down

at your feet and kiss the hem of your dress!
And what a pretty dress it is, and how
sweetly serious you look in it!"   And here,
somehow, there came into his head those lines
of Lamb's " To Hester.")

"What can we do more than we have done
already?" resumed Mr. Eliot.   "Our adver-
tisements are regularly repeated, but nothing
comes of them.   Inspector Coleby can gather
no clue, although he assures me some of his
best men have been set to work in the matter.
Sometimes I fancy the lad has enlisted, or left
the country—(you remember my telling you
that conversation his friend Mr. Swift repeated
to me)—or I fear a worse thing still.   Who
can say what despair might not drive him to!"

"Oh, no, *no*, Mr. Eliot!" broke in Margaret, vehemently.   "You must not have
such terrible thoughts!   I feel so sure that
your son will be heard of before long!   There
are many things, I know, a girl cannot see

as a man may; but I do believe I can understand the impulse that made him go away.
Somewhere or other now he is feeling sorrowful for the past, and resolving bravely for the
future; and by-and-by he will come back
to you and tell you everything; and it will
all be as though he had never left you!"

"God grant it, my dear!" said Mr. Eliot.
"But there — let us talk no more of the
matter at present. If you'll excuse me, I'll
go and see whether Alicia will not come downstairs. Dale, you'll stop dinner, of course?
There'll be one, I believe, when the children
are gone. Boddyman is coming in to us from
The Rectory."

Left, for the time being, alone with Miss
Oglevie, Dale was conscious of a something
which would have been satisfaction, but that
a certain embarrassment qualified the feeling.
This provoked him. He was not used to the
sensation, and felt inclined to exclaim with

Macbeth, in his swift self-impatience, "Protest me the baby of a girl!" Margaret betook herself to her needlework—silks on a ground of pale brown canvas, whereover three blue-green herons trailed forlornest legs above four bulrushes and a reed; perspective Chinese; general effect, a bath-towel illustrated. Woman has a receptive intellect, and Miss Oglevie had been told that here was Art pure and simple. We believe it was said to be "suggestive," or "subtle," or both.

Presently, with an external air, at least, of consummate ease, Mr. Dale began to speak.

"I didn't know when I rode over to-day, I should have the pleasure of meeting you, Miss Oglevie. You are staying at The Leas, I suppose?"

"Just till to-morrow. But I have been staying here nearly a fortnight, before Christmas. And everybody was so good to me, I felt quite down-hearted at leaving."

" Ah ! that was the fortnight I had to pass in London. I only came back for Christmas."

" Had you a pleasant one ?"

" *Comme ça !* I was at Little Upton, you see, with the Allan Dales. Dear Theresa brought St. Bees down; and we also had young Mrs. Ariel from Waste Court, and her baby. Oh, that baby !"

" Wasn't it nice ?"

" No, nasty ! The fretfullest, flabbiest specimen of unmuscular Christianity you can imagine ! Then there was *la belle sauvage,* Miss Diana Farr, whom you know, I believe ?"

" I've seen her on a Sunday at the Cathedral, I fancy. A tall girl ?"

" Yes. Leonine eyes and tawny hair."

" Tawny ? Why, Mr. Dale, it's dark-brown !"

" Say mulligatawny, then. I know the

colour is peculiar; and there's a lot of it—
what novelists nowadays call 'a wealth of
hair;' meaning, one would imagine, hair in
which much money had been invested. But
it didn't make her at all proud, and she
talked to me about her ponies, and so on,
most affably. She wants a dog."

"And have you not given her one?"

"Well, no. I offered one of my little white
Pomeranian pups, but she objected that it
took so much trouble to keep clean. Then I
offered her *two*, hinting that she could send
one to wash with her—with the rest of her
things, you know—whilst she wore the other:
I mean had it in use."

Now, all this time, although speaking with
the fluency and *savoir parler* of a clever man
of the world, Mr. Dale's thoughts but partially
companioned his speech, passing beyond it,
diving under and flying over it, in rapid
swallow-flights of fancy. Nor was he content

with the turn the conversation had taken.
He fain would have made it more closely
personal; he wanted to talk with Margaret
of herself, of her cherished aims and interests
—and somewhat, it might be, of his own. If
only she would lift her eyes from those pre-
posterous birds—that leggy three, the discom-
fort of whose attitudes and general angularity
were absurdly suggestive of mediæval saints.
But could he bid her (as Valeria bids her
friend) to lay aside her "stitchery," and
straight become confidential? Hardly might
maidens be summoned thus! And so he talked
small talk, as we all must, even when thinking momentously and feeling deeply. We
give each other conventional greetings, saying
a scant "How d'ye do?" to this one, though
our heart-beats redouble, our pulses leap, at
meeting; or a brief "Good-bye" to that one,
when, were it good-bye in earnest, the after-
years would be empty, and our eyes sicken of

the sun. Thus the precious minutes, the *mollia tempora fandi*, passed away, and at the end of a quarter of an hour Charles Eliot re-appeared, bringing his wife with him.

CHAPTER VII.

AN ORTHODOX APPARITION.

EANWHILE, the guests of the day, the five Draycott children, were supposed to be disporting themselves in the garden. Instead of doing this, however, they had made off to a certain bench at the foot of the biggest of the elm trees, through which, and through the poplars to the left, the wind was beginning to moan ominously.

Seated here (the influence of Mr. Eliot's story strong upon them), they proceeded to regale themselves with legendary odds and ends from their favourite fairy-books, gradually, with the waning of the short December day, edging one another on to the borders of the ghostly.

At the moment we return to them, and find them huddled together in the blustering twilight, the shadows deepening around them, their subject of conversation was neither more nor less than the devil.

The introduction of this personage was mainly due to the study of a small volume, entitled "Quarles' Emblems," recently discovered by Dora Draycott on an upper shelf of the lumber-room at The Manor—a volume whereof Pope has said :

"The pictures for the page atone,
And Quarles is saved by beauties not his own."

The "beauties" found by the little Draycotts were, it must be admitted, of a rather dark and dubious cast, and the conclusion to be come to after seeing them is, that if the devil

be as black as he is painted by Quarles, he
must be very black indeed.

As a matter of fact, the Prince of Evil,
with horns, hoofs, and a flourishing tail, runs
riot through the work ; and the superstitious
Dora and her fellows (not knowing, as did their
cultured father, that nineteenth century science
reduces Satan to a cypher,) were fearfully and
wonderfully impressed by his appearance.

Just as the discussion had reached a point
when the small voices were bated to smaller
whispers, and the five little heads were beginning to glance uneasily over their respec-
tive shoulders, one of the group was observed
to point a trembling finger toward the path
that led from the highway to the house, the
while eyes and mouth opened and widened
in woful apprehension.

With a simultaneous movement, the cluster
of children turned their dismayed vision in
the direction thus ominously indicated, and

there beheld an apparition fairly calculated
to make their young blood freeze.

Close upon them, and coming ever closer,
was a large, towering figure, black from head
to foot—a figure which loomed through the
dusky shrubberies with an awful vagueness of
outline, a mysterious softness of step.

One moment did the horrified juveniles
remain spellbound ; the next a general *sauve
qui peut*—a tumultuous stampede ensued.
The nearest recognised asylum was the hen-
house, and thither, over bed and border,
rushed the panic-stricken fugitives, banging
and barring the door behind them.

Out of the stuffy, strong-smelling darkness
of this refuge arose a small quavering voice,
timidly breaking the tomb-like silence that
had succeeded the sudden and violent entry.

" Who—who's here ?   Are we all safe
here ?"

By the exhaustive process of calling (or

rather whispering) over their names, it was ascertained that the entire party was present, save one—the unhappy, ill-starred Ethel. Of this young lady it behoves us, therefore, to speak.

At the moment when the gruesome object of their terror was first detected, Ethel, like her companions, had turned and fled. Always, however, an unfortunate child, she had scarce made half-a-dozen steps ere her foot tripped against a stone and brought her headlong to the ground. Here she remained, like Caliban before Stephano, too scared to stir, and awaiting, with a sinking soul, the coming evil.

Through the swaying, creaking poplars the boisterous sea-bred wind rose to a shriek of triumph (so it seemed to poor Ethel), and the shrubs around her cowered sympathetically earthward in their abject fear. The urgency of her situation suggested prayer, but, so

overwhelming was the agitation of her mind,
that the nearest approach to a petition she
could recall was the multiplication-table;
and "three times seven are twenty-one,"
even though uttered and reiterated with
agonised fervour, could have no special appli-
cation to her position.

"Why, you silly, *silly* child! What in
the world are you lying there for? Come,
come! get up, for goodness' sake!"

So saying, the devil (if, indeed, it *was* the
devil) grasped her by the arm and lifted her
to her feet, and—such is the subtlety of the
serpent—even proceeded to wipe her nose.
Thus taken in hand, Ethel was perforce driven
to regard the being into whose clutches she
had fallen, and, looking up, recognised, to her
intense relief, not the realisation of one of
Quarles's emblematic "beauties," but the
portly rector of the parish, the Reverend
Paul Boddyman.

"O!" gasped Ethel, the colour rushing back to her cheeks ; "why, it's Mr. Boddyman."

"Of course it is," said the rector, "of course it is. Whatever, I should like to know, did you take me for ?"

"We took you for the devil," answered Ethel, promptly.

"Hush, hush, hush ! Little girls mustn't talk like that; it's not pretty."

"Well, we *did!*" said Ethel, positively. "And you *are* dressed like him—all in black, you know ! And the others are in the hen-house. They think you've taken me and eaten me up."

"Eaten you up, indeed ! Who, pray, was so wicked and foolish as to tell you the devil eats children up ?"

"Nurse Dixon. Last Sunday. She said he goes about like a roaring lion (O *my !*), seeking whom he may devour ! Does he ?"

Somewhat taken aback at this very literal

interpretation of the Scriptures, the Reverend
Boddyman adroitly avoided controversy by
bidding Ethel conduct him to the house,
which behest (calling on the way to release
her brothers and sisters from their durance
vile) she gladly fulfilled.

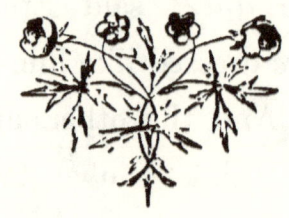

CHAPTER VIII.

UPPER STOREY STREET, SOHO.

THERE are a good many curious old houses in Soho, and, amongst them, No. 77, Upper Storey Street (at the corner of Queen Anne's Court), is as mouldy, worm-eaten, and time dishonoured as any. In No. 77 more than one family has taken up its abode. Size, the scene-painter, lives there; W. Buggins, waiter, lives there (please to ring the third bell, left-hand door-post); Monsieur A. Merveille, the dancing-master, lives there; little Nancy Fipps, the ballet-girl, and her grandmother, live there; Capps, the compositor ("who hath his quiver full of them "), lives there; and lastly, Edward East—in the attic—lives there.

Quoth the latter, waking at cock-crow, one January morning, to his friend and bedmate, Dick Eliot—

" Dick, have you got anything for breakfast ?"

" Yes."

Mr. East roused himself fully at this reply, gazed with an abstracted, anti-Brucean air at a spider overhead; and, having thoroughly realised the intelligence, spoke again.

" Is it enough for two, Dick ?"

" Yes."

Hope kindled and widened in Mr. East's blue eyes, and he gradually yielded himself up to the pleasures of anticipation. Fully five minutes elapsed before he ventured to dissolve the spell by making further inquiry.

" What have you got for breakfast that's enough for two, Dick ?"

" An appetite, Edward."

" Oh !"

At eight o'clock our hero jumped out of bed, and, so far as might be, dressed.

" Do you know, Ted, I've been thinking over what you said last night about trying my luck at writing again ; and, by Jove ! I'll begin to-day."

" Dick, shake hands ! If there's one man more than another certain to succeed in literature, it's yourself. Meanwhile, I'll finish that pen-and-ink sketch of Portia, and try to sell her as a pot-boiler. Thank heaven ! there's a little tobacco left, so we shall get along pretty comfortably without a fire. Light up, old fellow !"

The two young men, respectively representing art and literature, seated themselves on either side a bare, rickety table, Dick Eliot striving to embody his ideas in rhyme and rhythm, with a view to the periodical press ;

whilst his *vis-à-vis* laboured industriously at his etching of She of Belmont.

Does the reader comprehend the situation, or does he demand an explanation ?

When Edward East discovered our hero, half dead with want and exposure, in St. James's Park, he had been moved with compassion. All the Good Samaritanism of his kindly Bohemian nature woke into sympathetic life : and, as soon as Dick had given him an outline of his history, he had returned confidence for confidence, and finally proposed a union of their precarious fortunes.

The young artist's story was a simple one. Left an orphan (but otherwise left nothing at all) at an age when he most needed a parent's presence, Edward East was made over to the arid, unfruitful loves of distant relatives, who regarded the boy as a burden, and treated him accordingly. After being shifted from one cold household to another, he was finally taken charge of by his mother's cousin, the Reverend Gilead Barmecide, pastor and master of the Little Ebenezer Meeting-House, South Clapham.

This popular preacher was one of the most accomplished hypocrites that ever stood in pulpit instead of pillory. In him Pecksniff and Stiggins joined forces, whilst Tartuffe blessed the alliance. Something of the man's smooth, consummate villainy has been caught by Tennyson, who, with an imitation of Hudibrastic satire that comes like a breath of Butler from the underworld, pictures his prototype:

> " With all his conscience and one eye askew,
> So false he partly took himself for true !"

In the narrow-minded Methodistic circle of the Reverend Gilead Barmecide's admirers, Edward East became a sort of moral shuttlecock, and was tossed to and fro with unctuous

exhortation, spiritual warning, and blasphe-
mous assurance of eventual damnation, until
the fires of hell seemed to burn as continually
before the poor lad's eyes as the fires of Troy
before the eyes of Cassandra. Like Cassandra,
too, he must inevitably have gone mad with
horror of the future, but for one saving clause.
He fell in love—and the love of woman
(which is the love of God shown to man in its
tenderest form) revealed to him the existence
of goodness and gentle sympathy, of affection
and charity, and bade the half-smothered
hope in his bosom to breathe again.

East's captivator was a milliner's apprentice
—as pretty, confiding, and light-hearted a
little maiden as ever fought for bread-and-
butter at the needle's point. She lived with
her aunt in the neighbourhood of the Reverend Barmecide's Meeting-House, whereat
the puritanical tendencies of her senior com-
pelled her to attend. Here it was that she

first met with our friend Edward, who began
the acquaintance by offering her his hymn-
book, and improved it by offering her himself. Both were accepted—the former openly,
the. latter *sub rosâ;* and for a score or so
blissful Sundays they breathed their vows
over Clapham Common with the best of
them.

And then there came a frost, a killing frost,
which effectually nipped their young affections in the bud, and drove East from the
arms of his mistress, the milliner, to the
scanty caresses of his other mistress, Art.

One cloudless Sabbath evening, instead of
presenting themselves at the hot, stuffy little
chapel of their elders, where the Reverend
Barmecide—a very Milo of Methodists !—was
wrestling furiously with the Scarlet Woman,
they ventured to indulge their preference for
the open air and the beauties of surburban
nature. Their absence was noted by sundry

spinsters of the congregation, and officiously communicated to the Reverend Gilead, so soon as he had done preaching and perspiring. The heated pulpiteer turned his eyes heavenward in pious deprecation. A council was called; and in the front parlour of Miss Woodrow (our erring milliner's aunt) the awful elders and deacons of the Little Ebenezer Meeting-House awaited the appearance of the young people.

This was not until past ten o'clock! Edward East's voice was heard outside the window whispering farewell words to his sweetheart; and forthwith Miss Woodrow summoned him and her niece into the presence of the grim, unsympathetic tribunal. We will but attempt to indicate the scene that ensued. The Reverend Gilead,

> " Whose pious talk, when most his heart was dry,
> Made wet the crafty crowsfoot round his eye,"

mournfully declared that he had cherished " a

surpint in his buzzom;" and anon addressed the
trembling little Fanny as " a lost, abandoned
young wumman !"   Hereupon her lover interposed, flung prudence to the winds, and
" spake some certain truths " of the worthy
pastor, which rapidly brought matters to a
crisis.   Fanny was dismissed, sobbing, to her
bedroom ; Edward sent, with a storm of
honest indignation in his heart, uncere-
moniously out of the house.   That same
night he gathered together his small stock of
personal property, and quitted the roof of his
reverend relative, shaking the dust of Clapham
off his feet as he set his face Elephant-and-
Castlewards.

From this moment until the period at
which he now appears before the reader, he
had had a rather rough time of it.   The unbounded warmth with which he devoted himself to the worship of Art was not altogether
reciprocated, and he was in no little danger

of being sacrificed on her altar before he could win from her a single encouraging smile. Fortunately, his nature was a brave and persevering one. Hardship was wholly unable to mitigate his affections. Poverty came in at the door, but love did not fly out at the window ; and his only fluctuations were between the South Kensington Museum and the South Clapham milliner.

" Have you finished your poetry yet, Dick?" asked the young artist, tilting back his chair against the white-washed wall to obtain a bird's-eye view of his sketch.

" No ; not yet, confound it ! What's a rhyme to ' promise ?' "

" To ' promise ?' " murmured East, thoughtfully. " Bless me, how strange ! Why, I really can't think of one !"

" Nor can I. And I don't believe there is one—not a legitimate one, at least."

"'Thomas' wouldn't do, I suppose?" suggested East, deferentially.

"No, 'Thomas' won't do. Besides, it would be difficult to bring 'Thomas' in."

"Ah! I forgot that. Let's ask Nancy Fipps. She's just come back from rehearsal: I hear her on the stairs."

Dick smiled.

"Ask her if you like, Ted; but I don't think you'll get a rhyme, for all that."

A shrill voice was ascending from the ground-floor, singing clearly and resolutely a popular street-song of the period:

> "Try to be 'appy and gay, my boys!
> Remember the world is wide;
> Never to sorrow give way, my boys!
> But wait for the turn OF the tide."

"Nancy!" called East, looking down over the bannister outside the attic door.

"That's me," answered the shrill voice.

"I want to speak to you a moment, please."

27—2

"Comin' d'rectly, Mr. Heast. Just see if grandmother haven't burnt herself, or let the fire hout, and then I'll be with you."

In a few minutes the young lady made her appearance. A pretty, yellow-haired girl was Nancy Fipps, with a nose "tip-tilted" like Linette's; a girl always gay and good-humoured, and always ready alike to make or take a joke. A girl born and bred in poverty, but never repining at her lot, or disdaining the duties it involved. A good girl, too; and one who, although saying and doing a thousand things which would shock the sensibilities of her social superiors, was as really virtuous as the most immaculate of her sex.

There are many such young women in London—many more than you, O! sceptic, may imagine—and, indeed, it is only in London, amongst its milliners, dressmakers, models, ballet-dancers, bootbinders, and machine-hands, that one finds them to perfection. Here they may be met with by the hundred—neat, pretty, and unaffected; happy in the possession of the smallest bit of new finery, and wearing their unpretending little ribbons, and cuffs, and collars with as much good taste as ever a lady in the land. *Vidi tantum.*

Dick Eliot rose as their fellow - lodger entered the attic, and offered her his chair.

" Good-mornin', Mr. Heliot. Hawful cold, ain't it ? And, O my gracious ! you haven't got no fire !"

Before the gentlemen could make reply, or assure her that they never began fires until after Valentine's Day, the young person had stepped out of the room, whence, however, she speedily returned, with a dustpan full of burning coals in one hand, and a great piece of wood (lately a portion of the bannister) in the other. Laughing and talking, she knelt down before the narrow grate, blew the smouldering fire into a blaze, pulled forth a *London Journal* from her pocket and made a fan of it, and finally sat herself triumphantly on the edge of the bed, flushed with success, and breathless with enacting the part of bellows.

"'Pon my word, Nancy, you're a regular household fairy!" said East, looking gratefully at the little ballet-girl.

"No, I ain't," answered Nancy, smiling; "I'm honly a pantermine fairy. And O my! *such* a pantermine we're 'aving at the Paragon this year!"

"What's it called?" asked Dick, drawing his chair to the fire. "*Cock Robin Hood,* isn't it?"

"'*Cock Robin 'Ood; or 'Arlequin I said the Sparrer with my Bow and 'Arrer!*'" repeated Nancy, proudly. "And Miss Melville, she's second columbine, you know; and hold Methusaleh—(that's the ballet-master; we call him Methusaleh 'cause he wear a wig and beat his wife)—he say he'll put me in the front row next week, 'stead of 'Liza Hopkins !"

"And what does 'Liza Hopkins say ?" inquired Dick.

"She ? Oh, she say don't I wish I may get it ; and I say yes ; and then she say hold Methusaleh's a hold hidiot, and ain't heven fit to teach bears dancin'; which is a wicked story, 'cause he *is !*"

Dick laughed at the *naiveté* of this testimony to the ballet-master's merits ; and Nancy, finding him interested in her gossip of professional sayings and doings (which she dearly loved to dwell on), glibly continued talking.

"I suppose," questioned Dick, "you're not very busy at the Paragon just now, with the pantomime fairly in swing, and likely to keep going ?"

"Oh, but we are, though—no hend ! Mam'-

selle — (Mam'selle Zelzah, you know, our manageress)—mean to withdraw *Cock Robin 'Ood* at the beginnin' of next month, and we're all 'ard at it gettin' hup a new hextravaganza — *Cleopatrer; or the Sauce of the Nile.* Such a swell piece ! Mam'selle takes Cleopatrer of course ; and Miss Fanny Lancaster she plays Charmin."

" Plays charming, does she ?" repeated East, innocently.

" Yes ; Cleopatrer's lady's - maid, you know."

" Oh !" said Dick, smiling ; " Charmian ! And who, pray, is Miss Fanny Lancaster ?"

" Well, Mr. Heliot, that's almost more than I can tell you. Our ' additional attraction ' we call her. She come to us, about two month ago, from the provinces ; and some of our ladies say she's a relation of hold mother Thingmejig, the boxkeeper. Hanyhow, Lancaster ain't her real name ; it's honly the one she'll play hunder. And I was told she'd never so much as been on the boards before, till we 'ad her ; but that's a little more than this child can swaller. For oh ! she do act proper !"

" Which is what one can't say of every burlesque actress," remarked Dick, slily. " I must try and come to see her some night."

" I would, if I was you," said Nancy. " If there should be any ' paper ' goin', I'll get you and Mr. Heast a horder for the pit— hadmit bearer and friend, you know. I'm pretty well sure we shall make a 'it with the piece. There are some rattlin' good songs in it ; 'specially that one of Cleopatrer's, ' What Isis I stick to !' and the chorus belongin', ' With my Pyramiddy, idd-iddy, iddy-iddy- ay, Ri-pyramiddy-ol-dol-day !' Miss Lan- caster, too, has a hawful good duet with Mam'selle, and nicely savage Miss Melville have been about it. But there, it's no use

being jealous ; for when once Mam'selle takes
a fancy for a person, there's nothin' she won't
do for her—so long as it last."

"And has she taken a fancy for Miss
Lancaster, then ?"

"A fancy, Mr. Heliot! Fancy ain't no
word for it. Why, ever since she come to the
theatre Mam'selle 'ave been 'avin' her trained
and tootered, and showed this and learned
that, and made more fuss of than a little.
But to do the girl justice, she's a born actress,
and no mistake about it ! The other hevenin',
when Mam'selle brought Lord Langsyne behind with her (as she often do), I heard her
say to him, ' Fanny Lancaster ! Ah, she's as
like what our little Mary would 'ave been as
two peas!' and his Lordship says ' Oh !' (looking 'ard at 'er) ' and pray would our little
Mary 'ave been like two peas ?' and Mam'selle
turns round on him quick as quick, and calls
him a brute ; and he twisted 'old of his

moustache and said nothin'. But he seemed hupset somehow, and when one of the scene-shifters haccidentally ran against Polly Brown —hold Methusaleh's little girl—and 'urt her foot, he swore at him most hawful, and give Polly a kiss and a 'arf-crown."

At this point a remark from East turned the conversation into a new channel ; but, had Dick divined (as possibly the intelligent reader has already divined) that the subject they abandoned, Miss Fanny Lancaster, was none other than his old acquaintance Phœbe Langham, he might not so lightly have let it pass. But not even the faintest suspicion of this fact suggested itself ; and, inasmuch as he knew nothing of Phœbe's flight from Abingdon, it is perhaps, quite natural.

Upwards of an hour went by in desultory conversation, and then Nancy was summoned away by the querulous voice of her grand-mother to the room below.

"Ted," said our hero, "what's a rhyme to 'promise?'"

"By Jingo! Dick, I quite forgot to ask! Never mind. Look here! I've finished my Portia, and I'll take her to that place in Holborn and try and sell her."

"But it's raining, Ted, isn't it? Let me go. A fellow is always modest about his own work, and I shall be safe to make a better bargain with the dealer than you."

"No, no! You stop here and keep up the fire; then, you see, I shall be able to dry myself when I come back. Don't be getting glum, old man, while I'm away! Think of those lines you said Miss Ogleby——"

"Oglevie, Ted."

"Miss Oglevie told you; and hold on for the bright time that's coming. Good-bye, Dick!"

"Good-bye, Ted; and good luck, too."

Aroused by his comrade's parting words,

Dick put aside the verses at which he had been hammering throughout the morning, and essayed something in a lighter vein. Resolutely regarding the more humorous side of the situation in so lowly, lofty a garret as that they occupied, and bent on extracting from it such *lux e tenebris* as was possible, he set to work on a piece of rhyme, whereof the opening lines struck the key-note:

> "' What pleasure lives in height ?' quoth one
> · —The laureate of our isle.
> Ah, well ! we're first to see the sun
>   Who sleep beneath the tile :
> And he that cannot glean from it
>   Some hope, I hold to fault ;
> And he that hath no ' attic ' wit
>   Not worth his ' attic ' salt !"

CHAPTER IX.

ART IN EXTREMIS.

WHEN, some two hours later, Edward East returned to his friend, he found him aglow with the satisfaction of effort and achievement; for in these days, ere yet his pen had become hackneyed and over-facile, our hero experienced a relish in writing, wholly apart from any consideration merely mercenary.

"Dick, you villain! put away those papers; you've worked long enough. Look here! Do you see this? It's a shilling. Run to the Cat and Fiddle, next door, and get a pot of half-and-half. And Dick!—just ask the

barmaid to give us a little mustard in a piece
of paper. And Dick!—two screws of best
bird's-eye. And Dick——"

But Dick Eliot had deftly caught the coin
East tossed him, and was already half-way
downstairs in quest of beer and 'bacca.
During his absence the young artist spread a
sheet of newspaper over the table, produced
from under his coat a half-quartern loaf, and
from his breast-pocket a small packet of cold
boiled beef. These he carefully disposed with
an eye to effect, adding a knife and a pair of
two-pronged forks from the cupboard over
the door. From this recess he also evoked
an empty ginger-beer bottle, in the neck of
which he stuck a candle of the genus *dip*,
lighted it, and drew the table close up to the
fireside. His next act was to suspend the
counterpane curtain-wise across the window;
and, finally, having replenished the fire with
a further fragment of the bannister, he

sat himself down to await his friend's return.

"Here you are, Ted!" exclaimed Dick, entering the attic a minute or so later. "A pot of half-and-half, fivepence; two screws of best bird's-eye, threepence—that's eightpence; mustard, gratis; and change, fourpence—that's a shilling. Why, hullo! what's this? Boiled beef, as I'm a living sinner! '*Bene ego nunquam*—well I never!' What a brick you are, East! Take a pull at the beer, and then tell me about your picture-sale. Now then!"

"All right, Dick; wait a second, and you shall hear everything. Good beer, isn't it?"

"Awful! Capital beef, too, by Jove! Where did you get it?"

"Corner cook-shop, up the court. Nancy Fipps deals there. Mustard, please."

"Beg pardon! After you with the knife.

What first-rate bread the bakers sell nowadays—haven't you noticed?"

"Astonishing! Oh, they are good fellows,
those bakers, let people say what they
will."

"Yes; so are barmaids. Fancy! that one
next door, who gave us the mustard, wanted
me to take some salt as well! Jolly of her,
wasn't it?"

"Very. Pity her nose is so out of drawing, though! Were there many people in
the bar? Size? Was Size there?"

"Yes, Size was there—as usual."

"Drunk?"

"Dead!"

"*Dead?*"

"Dead-drunk, I mean; or 'mortally in-
ebriated,' if you like that better. What's in a
name? A Size by any other name would be
as screwed. There! Thank God for a good
meal! How do you feel now, Ted?"

" I feel," said East, impressively, " I feel
' like a giant refreshed with wine, and rejoicing as a strong man to—to—' How does
that quotation conclude, Dick ?"

" ' To run a-muck,' " answered Dick,
gravely.

" Yes ; thanks ! ' And rejoicing as a strong
man to run a-muck.' Well ! now light up,
and I'll tell you about my picture."

" Do."

Thus encouraged, Edward East proceeded
to relate how he had gone to the place in
Holborn, and been repulsed ; how he had
then tried his luck at a shop in Gray's Inn
Road, the proprietor of which had turned up
his nose at Portia, and inquired if he had got
" nuffin' from the nood ? a Wenus, a Leader,
or a Hariadney ?" how he had next wandered
into Oxford Street, and how here success had
at length attended him, and his etching been
disposed of for three half-crowns. All this,

and the additional fact of a companion sketch of Nerissa having been entrusted him, did Edward East exultantly narrate, Dick Eliot thoughtfully puffing his pipe, and dropping occasional remarks of astonishment or assent by way of evincing his interest in the story.

Shortly after eleven the two friends turned into bed, having previously economically raked out the remnant of their fire. Dick dozed off almost immediately, but was aroused between three and four in the morning by a gleam of light and the muffled paddling of stockinged feet about the chamber.

"Are you awake, Dick?" said East's voice, in a whisper.

"Yes. What's the matter?" cried Dick, starting up.

"Why, I've got a most extraordinary idea for a sketch—quite an original idea!—but, you see, I want a model. Be a model, will you, old fellow ?"

" Yes," said our hero, slowly; " certainly."

So he got out of bed, and became a model —putting first his legs into the full light of the candle, and then his head and shoulders—Edward East working away enthusiastically at his sudden inspiration in all earnestness and simplicity.

A few nights afterwards the small hours were again signalised by a similar episode, and by degrees Dick Eliot became fully accustomed to the whispered " Be a model," of his artistic companion, and was wont to lend a hand (or a foot, as the case might be) almost mechanically.

Thus the winter went by.

CHAPTER X.

FRIENDS IN NEED.

R. OSCAR DALE was in London. A series of sharp frosts had rendered hunting hopeless, and life at Idlewild, apart from such outdoor distractions, did not greatly commend itself to him. Besides, he liked London, having all Lamb's or Johnson's relish for Fleet Street and the Temple, of which neighbourhood he had aforetime been a recognised frequenter. Prior, indeed, to his uncle's death, whilst yet a young man of limited means, he had occupied chambers in Lincoln's Inn Fields; and between these and airy apartments *au troisième* in Continental hotels, his time had mainly been divided. Although at no period relying on his pen for a livelihood, Mr. Dale had been wont to add to his income by occasional contributions to magazines and reviews; and hence had arisen an acquaintance with many men of letters, with the interiors of studios, and the unpainted side of theatrical scenery.

For in these earlier days he was of Bohemia, Bohemian; a bird of passage, indeterminate as Browning's Waring; and although editorial chiefs were conscious that the initials " O. D.," in the pages of periodicals, were invariably preceded by some article at once pungent and pithy, they were also conscious that the owner of these initials was too independent, too unpunctual, and prone to pleasure, to be trusted as a regular contributor. " A most promising writer!" said Scrubb, the critic of the

Weekly Wash, to Sudds, its editor. "*Most* promising," growled Sudds, sardonically; "and that's the devil of it! If he were a little less full of promise, and a little more given to performance, I'd be better pleased, Mr. Scrubb—much better pleased; and so I shall tell him."

Ab uno disce omnes. Sudds was not the only one who waited for Dale's "copy," or who sware in his wrath to go to press without it—which, by-the-way, he was seldom in a position to do. Brown, of the *Morning Call*, and Jones, of the *Evening Party*, were equally victims of his Fabian policy; whilst as for De Witt of the *Laughing Jackass* (comic rival of the *Merry-Andrew*), he would keep a boy by the hour together at an upper window of his office in Fleet Street, to report, "Sister Anne-wise," whether or no Dale could be seen approaching to his overdue appointment.

De Witt, moreover, whose sense of the fit-

ness of things had been so perverted by a
long course of comic journalism that he was
wont to make fun of himself, as well as of
other people, ingeniously parodied a well-
known passage of "Enoch Arden," in allu-
sion to his contributor's shortcomings.   As
thus :

> " No Dale from day to day, but every day ,
>   The newsboys running by the scarlet shafts
>   Of hansom cabs, 'mong carts and omnibuses ;
>   The roaring of the traffic to the east ;
>   The roaring of the traffic underneath ;
>   The roaring of the traffic to the west ;
>   Then the great ' stars' that write the morning leaders,
>   The hollower-rumbling ' Pickfords,' and, again,
>   The scarlet shafts of hansoms—but no Dale !"

All this, however, belongs to the past.
At present Mr. Dale had taken up his
quarters at the Charing Cross Hotel, which
he found conveniently intermediate between
the world of the West End and that other
world he had sojourned in of old.

Meanwhile our hero and his friend, East,

continued lingering—not living—in their Upper Storey Street eyrie. Since last we saw them, Dick Eliot had gained his first guinea in payment for a poem in a monthly magazine. With this, and the sale of a sketch or two of East's, they had contrived to keep starvation at arm's length; but Famine was always dodging and sparring round them, seeking for an opening to get beneath their guard.

One day Dick swore that he could stand it no longer, and seized his hat with the avowed intention of going into Westminster to enlist as a soldier.

"I shan't be the first poor devil of a poet who's had to do the like," said he, moodily, to his fellow-lodger. "Colley Cibber did so; Coleridge did so; Edgar Poe did so; and— and heaven knows who else!"

East opposed his determination most strenuously.

" Never mind what *they* did ; don't you be such a fool, old fellow ! Things ain't quite so bad as that yet. At least, let's try to hold out a little longer. Look here ! If nothing turns up within a week, why I'll go with you, and we'll be miserably military together."

Nancy Fipps, overhearing something of this discussion, and guessing at the rest, came and added her arguments to those of the young artist, and did more with her clear common-sense and downright speech than anything else. Dick Eliot agreed to wait a week ; but, ere a half of that time had elapsed, a gleam of light had appeared on the horizon.

CHAPTER XI.

DALE'S FIND.

I T was a Wednesday evening—a wet Wednesday evening, and the scene was the West End. A dull, pepper-castor of a cloud had been sprinkling London since the early morning, and now that night had set in, it had thickened into a steady March drizzle. Metropolitan out-door life was divided into two distinct classes— those who had umbrellas, and those who had none. Let us take a specimen of each.

A young man *without* an umbrella. A shabby young man, with a closely-buttoned frock-coat, trousers very much frayed at

the bottoms, and boots whose tread on the
pavement is suspiciously noiseless, suggesting
brown-paper soles, and socks (if any) sodden
with rain. A pale, sharp-featured young
man, hungry of eye and haggard of expression. A young man with unusually small,
well-formed hands, and, despite his attire, the
air of a gentleman. A young man having
under his arm a parcel containing fish (that
is to say, two herrings in a piece of newspaper), and in his coat-pocket a cottage loaf.
A young man whose name is Eliot, and whose
destination is an attic in Soho.

A young man *with* an umbrella. Rather a
well-dressed individual, this one; dainty of
linen, shiny of boot, and cultivated of moustache. He stands at the doorway of what
was then Mr. E. T. Smith's restaurant, at the
corner of Leicester Square, whence he has
just emerged from the society of bitter beer
and anti-bitter barmaids. His name is Dale,

and he is hesitating whether to have a hansom back to Charing Cross, or not.

A slight thing decides him. Young man No. 1, passing the doorway where he stands, is cannoned against by a market-gardener, and incontinently drops his parcel on the pavement. Young man No. 2, acting on impulse, picks it up, and, seeing its owner unconscious of his loss, considerately hurries after him to restore it.

"I beg your pardon, but you've dropped your—evening paper," said Dale, politely ignoring the existence of the fish it enfolded.

"Eh? Ah, thanks, thanks! Its herrings."

"Oh, herrings! Yes; of course. But I *say*——!"

"Dale!"

"Good God! it *is* Dick! Dick, my dear old fellow, what in the world does this mean? Oh, you sinner! you sinner! But there,

don't attempt to talk—let's have a cab, and
you come straight off home with me at once.
Bless'd if we don't get a special!"

"No, no, Dale. I—I can't. I've a friend
waiting for me at my own lodging. This is
our dinner, you see, and——"

But here his voice abruptly failed him.
The sight of an old home-face brought up
such a flood of memories of a gracious past,
that the present seemed doubly black and
detestable by contrast. In that moment he
tasted the utmost bitterness of his fallen
fortunes. All the wretchedness, the mean-
ness, the vulgarity of poverty was realised as
he turned his head from his friend to hide
the sharpness of his distress. All the
coarseness of his daily surroundings; all the
absence of those numberless small graces and
refinements which to an organisation such as
his were well-nigh necessities of life; all the
bareness and repulsiveness of a hand-to-

mouth existence; all the mental and physical suffering he had undergone—all crowded to his mind with the sudden recognition of Oscar Dale, and, for the moment, choked the utterance in his throat.

As to Dale, he was a thoroughly good fellow, and felt pained to the heart to find his friend in such a miserable plight.

"Oh, d——n it!" muttered he, looking intently at a tub of "Best Fresh," in an adjacent cheesemonger's, in order to give Dick time to recover himself; and when he began speaking, he assumed a charitable ignorance of his companion's emotion, rattling on with cheerful volubility, and with a carelessness he was far from feeling.

"All right, Dick! If the mountain won't come to Mahomet, Mahomet 'll come to the mountain. You shall take me with you. Nonsense! why not? Oh, and we shall want some more herrings. I'm as hungry as a hunter. See! there's a place yonder; let's go and buy some."

So saying he seized hold of Dick's arm, crossed over to the shop he had indicated, nodded affably to the proprietor, and demanded " half - a - dozen pure and simple bloaters."

" Do you fancy a 'ard roe or a soft roe, sir ?"

" Well, I don't know. I think I should like a good Front Row ; or a Wild Mountain Roe ; or some of the Last Roes of Summer. Or stop! these will do. Half-a-dozen—right! *Combien ?* as the immortal Voltaire once (or twice) remarked. Ninepence ? Thanks. *Good evening.*"

Before reaching Upper Storey Street, Dale insisted on halting to purchase a variety of eatables and drinkables of the most incongruous description—from jars of preserved meat and cocoanuts to Irish whisky and

Scotch marmalade. Passers-by stared at the two young men with their multiplicity of parcels; at the trembling lip and shabby appearance of the one, at the eager eyes, sympathetic regard, and gentlemanly "get-up" of the other.

In a measure, Dale could divine from our hero's general aspect, from outward and visible signs, the dolefulness of his history since seeking London. But one thing rather perplexed, perturbed him. In the first agitation of their encounter, Dick had spoken of a friend awaiting him and his herrings at the lodgings in Soho. Who could this friend be, this nameless partner of his dinner and dwelling? Surely, surely not that girl from Abingdon — that "billiard - sharper at the Goose of Gideon," as Mrs. Towle persistently described her. Heaven forbid! But what if Dick's folly had been greater, his infatuation more

fatal, than they had hitherto credited ? Was
it possible, after all, that Charles Eliot's son
should have formed a *liaison*, or made a
mésalliance, so wofully compromising ? The
thought was confusion ; but the truth must
be known, and the sooner it was elicited the
better.

" By - the - way, you mentioned someone
waiting for you, didn't you, Dick ?" quoth
Mr. Dale, with assumed indifference. "Who's
your friend ?"

" My friend ? Ah, Dale ! my friend is one
you must all make welcome, and learn to like
for my sake."

"The devil we must !" ejaculated Dale,
vehemently. " O Lord ! so the young fool
is married, after all, then ! Dick, Dick ! this
is too much—this is worse than we feared !
I had rather have lost a fortune, almost,
than have learnt this thing of you. How
am I to tell your father ? What do you

suppose your poor mother will say to such a wife ? It's awful !"

Dick stopped abruptly, staring in amazement.

" A wife ! In the name of goodness, what are you talking of ? I *married !* Why, I'm no more married than yourself !"

" Then, damn it, sir, you ought to be !" cried Mr. Dale, sharply. " Look here, Richard Eliot ! I'm no strict moralist—never was ; but, by Jove ! when a mere lad like you coolly——."

Here Dick interposed.

" Dale, I don't understand you one bit ! What *ever* is it all about ? First, you flare up because you seem to imagine I'm married, and the next moment you flare up worse because I tell you I'm not married. Please explain."

Oscar Dale looked at him keenly.

29—2

" How about that poor girl from Abingdon, Dick ?"

" What girl ! You don't mean Phœbe Langham, do you ?"

" Phœbe Langham — that's the name ! Where is she, Dick ?"

" Where ? Why, at Abingdon, I suppose. Where else should she be ?"

" Then she's not here with you in Soho ?"

" Phœbe Langham here with me ! You must be mad, Dale ! Phœbe Lang—— Why, bless you ! there's nobody with me but Edward East, the friend I spoke of. What in the world put such a notion in your head?"

And now, for the first time, Dick Eliot learned the tidings of Phœbe's flight from Abingdon, and how promptly and plausibly scandal had associated her disappearance with his own. The news confounded him. With a flash of retrospective thought, he grasped the full sense of the situation, and saw to what grievous misinterpretation the rumour must have exposed him.

"Tell me, Dale," said he, after a pause, " did my father believe this of me?"

" No, he didn't," answered Dale; " nor your mother, nor I either. But, you see, lots of people did, Dick."

Dick's face flushed.

" Everybody, I suppose," muttered he, bitterly, " except you three!"

"You're wrong there, old fellow! Miss Oglevie, for one, stood out for you like—like —well! like the true heart she is."

Dick's lips trembled, but he spake no word. For a minute the two walked on in silence; then, in response to a question of Dale's, his companion began, bit by bit, to disburden himself of the story of his life since leaving Oxford. By the time Upper Storey Street

was gained, Mr. Dale had managed to glean
a fragmentary abridgment of his adventures
in London; and presently they were both
groping their way up the dark rat-riddled
staircase of No. 77, to the topmost floor of
the house. But prior to thus quitting the
lower world, a telegram had been despatched
to Charles Eliot, at The Leas.

East was down on his knees before the
hearth, like a fire-worshipper, when they
entered the attic, and failed to hear their
approach. As he puffed the glowing embers
into flame, there were some wonderful effects
of flickering light and shade about the gaunt,
whitewashed walls and heavy cobwebbed
rafters of the garret, which, as a " study of
an interior," might well-nigh have evoked
Rembrandt, or old Godfrey Schalken, into
artistic life again.

Dale and East took to each other with
unaffected cordiality. The kindly wit and

easy good-fellowship of the one, and the simplicity and quiet courage of the other, afforded a mutual attraction. Before an hour had passed they were on the best terms imaginable.

CHAPTER XII.

EVENTS IN AN ATTIC.

AFTER a meal of the most miscellaneous and dyspeptic character (during which Dick, in his eagerness to appease hunger, had nearly shared the fate of poor Otway under similar circumstances), the " divine weed " and the no less divine whisky were freely circulated. Once again, for the first time since several months, did our hero experience a sense of comfort. The nicotine soothed him; the alcohol strengthened him; the society of Dale enlivened him. His old self, animated and enthusiastic, showed signs of revival.

As there are cunning chemically-prepared pictures, whose colours appear faint, or else are wholly invisible, until held to the warmth and glow of the fire, so it is with certain men. A cold atmosphere enfeebles, nullifies, or even destroys them ; nor is it till they encounter the influence of light and comfort that their latent qualities are revealed.

In frankest, friendliest converse the evening hours wore away. Dick had a thousand questions to ask of Dale, and as many to answer. Once or twice Edward East was fain to have withdrawn and left the two friends by themselves, but neither would hear of his leaving them ; and shortly after eleven their company was further increased by the appearance of Nancy Fipps.

" Hullo ! Who comes so late ?" exclaimed Mr. Dale, hearing a foot upon the threshold.

" Honly me," said Nancy, hesitating at

the doorway. " I didn't know as you'd got company, Mr. Heliot."

" An' if a' be called company, may I be hanged !" quoth Dale, *sotto voce.*

" Oh, come in Nancy. Don't be afraid : it's nobody."

" Gin I be named nobody, may I be set i' the stocks for a vagabond ! Dick, you sinner, don't deprecate your visitor."

" This is Mr. Dale, Nancy—one of the best fellows in Christendom ; and this, Dale, is Miss Fipps—one of the prettiest girls in Christendom, or Jewry either !"

" Please be quiet, Mr. Heliot, or I shan't come and say good night hany more."

" Here's a seat, Nancy," said East. " Sit down, and warm yourself. Why, you're quite wet !"

" Oh, that's nothin' ! I forgot to take my humbrella with me this hevenin', and it was rainin' when we left the theatre, as per usual."

So saying, the little ballet-dancer sat herself down before the fire, placed her feet on the fender, and demurely turned her dress back over her knees in order to dry her damp petticoats.

" Miss Fipps, you must drink out of my glass," said Dale. " My grog is the sweetest and hottest, and it will save you from catching cold."

Nancy accepted the offer with a smile of thanks ; the conversation was made general, and morning found them still laughing and talking round the attic fire—

> "Merry as when nuptial day is done
> And tapers burn to bedward !"

Here we can imagine the reader—the " gentle " reader—flinging the book down in disgust. My dear Sir, or dearest Madam, wherefore ? Doth our little bit of undraped Bohemianism offend thee ? Is this innocent attic-orgie an abomination in thy sight? Shall there be no more cakes and ale, no more singing and dancing, save in decent society? What *is* decent society? ("Aha!" shrieks Thersites, coming from his hiding-place round the corner, "he doesn't know! he doesn't know!") And what, oh! what is Bohemianism?

Why, too, should the term "Bohemian" be a term of reproach? Do ye know, O ye immaculate men and women! ye who have no faults except one—"the fault of not being great enough to commit any"—do ye know how many of our mightiest have been Bohemians in their youth? how many, like mad Prince Hal, have dwelt with unworthy company in stews and taverns, ere they came forth to win battles and the world's hand-clapping?

When, for instance, a young man of respectable parents and good education joins in drinking bouts and poaching frolics, makes a foolish, if not a forced marriage in his teens, with a woman seven or eight years his senior, leaves his home for London, where, peradventure, he holds horses at play-house doors, shall we not brand him as a Bohemian? Certainly, by all means. Very well. Only, by-and-by, our tongues are stopped, for, lo and behold! this good-for-nothing young man has made himself immortal as William Shakspere.

Here, again, are two more Bohemians—miserable Bohemians these—shivering under Temple Bar at midnight, bedless and breadless. But, hereafter, the world learns of these outcasts as Samuel Johnson and Richard Savage.

Oliver Goldsmith, living "in Axe Lane among the beggars," or about to marry his landlady in Green Arbour Court, as Dufresney married his laundress, because he could not

pay her bill, was an arrant Bohemian. And
yet he gave us the " Vicar of Wakefield."

Crabbe, we suppose, was a Bohemian until
Burke told people he was something more ;
and Gifford, cabin-boy and cobbler, was perforce a Bohemian ere he became editor of the
Quarterly. How, too, about Thackeray, the
student of the *Quartier Latin*, who dedicated
his first-fruits to his tailor, in acknowledgment of " money lent ?" and what of the child
Charles Dickens (loneliest of little ones !),
covering blacking-pots and starving on a
salary of six shillings a week ?

And you, ladies and gentlemen, you eye
these Bohemians askance ; turn up your noses
at their garret beginnings ; sneer at their
associations ; and, " content to dwell in
decencies for ever," speak of their unconven-
tional existence with sanctimonious deprecation. You thank God that you are not as
these others, publicans and sinners ; and

mistake a simply prosaic life for a pious one.

> " She had lived, we'll say,
> A harmless life (*she* said a virtuous life) ;
> A quiet life which was not life at all :
> But that she had not lived enough to know."

Peace, ye British Philistines, peace ! Let the Bohemian alone ! Leave him to himself, to his books, and (gif the gods be gracious) to his beer and 'bacca ! Or, an' ye have wit enough to be sarcastic, say unto him as Launcelot said unto Jessica : " I always was plain with you, and so now I speak my agitation of the matter ; therefore be of good cheer, for truly I think you are damned."

* * * * *

Next morning before noon, Charles Eliot had reached town, and, taking a hansom ("the gondola of London," as Mr. Disraeli terms it), directed the driver to the Charing Cross Hotel. Here he found Mr. Dale, and

together they proceeded to Upper Storey
Street, Soho.

"How does he seem, Dale?" asked Mr.
Eliot, eagerly. "Is he well? Tell me!"

So Dale told him all that he had heard
from Dick, and Charles Eliot listened in
silence. In ten minutes the cab stopped at
No. 77.

Oscar Dale, running up the stairs to the
attic in advance of his companion, whom he
left to settle with the cabman, put his head in
at the door and nodded a greeting.

East was standing in the middle of the
chamber, his legs planted well apart, polishing
a decrepit boot with a brush whose bristles
were "scant as hair in leprosy." Dick sat at
the table, nervously nibbling the end of his
pen.

"'Morning, boys, morning! Mr. East, I
just want a word with you, please; if you'll
be kind enough to come out with me a minute

or two. Dick, old fellow, I've brought a visitor with me !"

East, divining whose arrival was thus heralded, impulsively hurled his brush among the rafters, and fervently exclaimed, "Thank God !" Then, drawing on his half-cleaned boot, he followed Dale from out the attic. On the stairs they encountered Mr. Eliot, to whom Nancy Fipps was pointing the way. He halted a second, looked at East earnestly, and held forth his hand.

"Thank you, Mr. East !" said he simply ; and so saying, passed on.

Dick heard his father's footstep on the stairs, and started from his seat. Then he stopped, trembling. With the moment's pause his past conduct seemed to rise up, sudden and sharp, and stand out clearly before his eyes; and a sense of shame and unworthiness overwhelmed him. He fell forward on his knees beside the table, his head

buried in his arms.   In a little while a hand
was laid upon his shoulder, and a voice said :

" Dick, look up !"

Only love, and pity, and pardon were in the
tones that reached him, and his heart felt like
to break.

" Dick, my boy, you will trust me another
time, won't you ?"

Then his father's arm was round him, and
he sobbed like a little child, knowing that his
troubles were over.

CHAPTER XIII.

FROM THE LEAS TO THE MANOR.

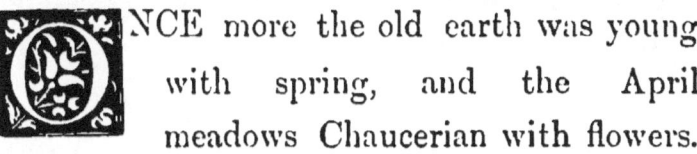NCE more the old earth was young with spring, and the April meadows Chaucerian with flowers. The budding hedgerows, that erewhile were bare, and dripping, and wind-worried, were now again delicious with promise, spreading and expanding their tender greenery, and soon to become such " liberal homes of unmarketable beauty " as make poets and farmers alike thoughtful—albeit, with different promptings.

Through these fresh woods and pastures new of the young year, Dick Eliot was wend-

30—2

ing his way on a certain April morning,
taking a cross-country route from The Leas
to Draycott Manor. After the squalid un-
loveliness of Soho, the dewy grace and purity
around him were inexpressibly sweet.

For months his soul had been starved of
beauty; and now, so keen was his sense of
the thrush's song, and the hyacinth's fragrance,
that he felt his heart within him' aching for
utterance, and thrilled with the divine pain of
poetry.

He had been home a fortnight, and in that
fortnight he had come fully to realise how
complete and generous was the affection his
parents bore him—how loyal was the regard
of such friends as Oscar Dale and Margaret
Oglevie. Not a single word or sign of reproach had reached him from any one or other
of these; and if Mrs. Towle had turned stony
eyes on him, and Miss Towle averted her
head, at a chance encounter, the implied

rebuke of matron and maid disturbed him but little.

Dick's walk to the Manor led through pleasant places. The gossip of building birds —"the melodious 'armony of fowles," as Dame Berners hath it—filled his ear as he passed by stream and woodland. Now a pair of white-throats, their plumage glancing like silver, would wing their way across his path; and now a willow-wren flitted before him, or a blackcap (that enemy of orchards!), with its wild fresh carol, would companion his flying thoughts for a field's length. Anon, too, came the word

> " In a minor third
> There is none but the cuckoo knows ;"

and once, from a near coppice, broke out, loud and true, the full-hearted song of the nightingale.

Dick was thinking, as he went, of Mar-

garet Oglevie, and wondering if he should
see her at the Manor or not.   Something had
been said, a day or two previous, of the
possibility of her coming thither on occasion
of the joint birthday of Dora and Tom, and
there was also a talk of her father dining
with Sydney Draycott on this anniversary.
It was no more than a chance rumour which
had reached him, but it was enough to decide
Dick on taking his presents to his twin
cousins in person, rather than intrusting
them to the hands of a servant.   For our
hero had come to consider a glimpse of
Margaret as worth an undetermined number
of miles' walk, an unknown quantity of
waiting and watching.   With a growing
appreciation of good and evil, a deeper sense
of life's problems and possibilities, there had
risen in his heart a fuller and clearer recognition of the beauty of Margaret's character.
And this recognition, whilst ever raising her

in his eyes, had the effect of humbling himself, insomuch that her purity and unselfishness were as a reproach to him, her noble maidenhood as a light that showed him whatsoever was blameful and unworthy in his own manhood. But although reverence was thus strong within him, love was yet stronger, and, by divine right of its royalty over all the passions that sway the hearts of men and women, took precedence and led the way. Dick thought of Margaret as a lover thinks, with pride and tenderness for the simplest of her womanly adornments—the flower at her breast, the ribbon binding her hair; treasuring in his memory a hundred trifling phrases and actions familiar to her; remembering how a loosened tress had looked against the oval of her cheek, how she had swept it back with her hand, and how pure and gracious was the curve of her face from ear to chin, thereby revealed to him.

Presently, leaping a stile into a lane beyond, Dick found himself brought face to face with a fellow-creature—the first he had encountered in his walk. This was Mr. Abbs, the Rev. Paul Boddyman's curate. Mr. Abbs was a young man whom Charles Eliot, quoting the phraseology of a popular advertisement, was wont to describe as "truly efficacious and mild." He was a very good young man, angelic to excess; and apparently, like the angels, of no sex. That is to say, he knew nothing of those masterful human passions whereby a man may haply find himself deified at night and damned on the morrow. Maiden ladies, growing and grown, would sit gazing upon the chaste and placid sweetness of Mr. Abbs' countenance in an ecstacy of quasi-religious adoration—a sort of pious and pithless spooniness inexpressibly irritating to a practical-minded person. To Dick Eliot, Mr. Abbs was specially provoking.

Firstly, because the Christian name he bore—
Richard—was identical with his own; secondly,
because he was persistently favoured by Miss
Oglevie, in whose presence our hero so continually found him, that he had begun to
speak of him, with humorous impatience, as
" that perpetual curate !"

" Beg pardon," said Dick, seeing that his
harlequin-like abruptness of entry into the
lane had somewhat discomposed the young
cleric, causing him to let fall what at first
looked like a kitchen candle-box, but was, in
reality, a botanist's specimen-case. "I didn't
mean to disturb you."

Mr. Abbs smiled sweetly—and Dick wished
he wouldn't.

" Pray, pray do not mention it, Mr.
Eliot !"

" Ah, but I *have*," muttered Dick, *sotto
voce.* Then aloud, " Fine day, isn't it ?"

" Beautiful ! beau-ti-ful !"

" Fern-hunting, I suppose ?"

" Excuse me—no. Not ferns, Mr. Eliot. Just a few green herbs of the earth, of the genus *Cardamine.* This, you see, is the *Cardamine Pratensis.*"

" Looks to me like a lady's-smock," said Dick, taking it in hand.

" Like a—er—I beg your pardon ?"

" A lady's-smock," repeated Dick, bluntly. " That's its name in English, you know. Shakspere mentions it somewhere."

Again Mr. Abbs smiled sweetly.

" 1 gathered as much from Miss Oglevie," observed he, pensively regarding the plant. " But I did not understand if the—er—the bard alluded to it by its botanical title, *Cardamine Pratensis,* or by—er—by the term you speak of."

"Yes, that's it," said Dick, absently. " By-the-way, Mr. Abbs, was it lately you saw Miss Oglevie ?"

" Last evening, Mr. Eliot ; I saw her last evening. And I am not unhopeful of seeing her to-day."

" Oh, indeed !"

" You see, she is greatly interested in the new Book Club we are seeking to form for our humbler brethren at Hethercote and the adjoining parishes. She has, indeed, presented many volumes toward our Library ; and has promised to obtain others. There are, among them, perhaps, works which are somewhat too secular in their tone—not affording such purely spiritual food as one might desire—but the committee, Mr. Eliot (whereof I rejoice to be a member), will doubtless retain those only that directly tend to the eternal welfare of the precious souls who—er—who become subscribers."

There was in Mr. Abbs' speech a certain glib blandness and admixture of clerical " shop," against which Dick Eliot inwardly

chafed ; and, for the moment, his sentiment
toward the curate might best have been
expressed by Orlando's words to Jacques—
" I do desire we may be better strangers."
Only his craving to learn more of the possible
movements of Margaret Oglevie prevailed on
him to prolong the interview, whereby he
eventually gathered that the young lady had
signified an intention of visiting Draycott
Manor in the course of the day, and (did
opportunity serve) of extending her visit to
Hethercote, in order that Mr. Abbs might
show her the books already collected for the
new club. Thus much information gained,
our hero shortly bade the curate good morning, and pursued his walk.

Following the lane (the same wherein, a
spring gone by, Ulric Drummond had
declared himself to Lydia Brooke), Dick
presently sighted above the tree-tops the
clock-tower of Hethercote Hall. Change had

come hither, as elsewhere. "All our yester-
days have lighted fools the way to dusty
death." Poor old Sir Hugo was dead, and
Sir Ulric reigned in his stead ; for the
elder son had likewise met the common
fate of flesh, be it witty or witless, and
now slept with his forefathers in the family
vault ; Lady Muffle Drummond (the dow-
ager) and her daughters had thereupon
departed to town, betaking themselves to
one of those cramped but coveted mansions in
Park Lane; whilst Sir Ulric and his wife possessed the Hall. Here, in dubious harmony,
they dwelt together, studiously shunned
by the county, and only seeing beneath
their roof such bachelor intimates of the
husband as were flattered to receive his in-
vitations. Ralph Oglevie referred to them
as "the great unvisited."

CHAPTER XIV.

GODFATHER AND GODSON.

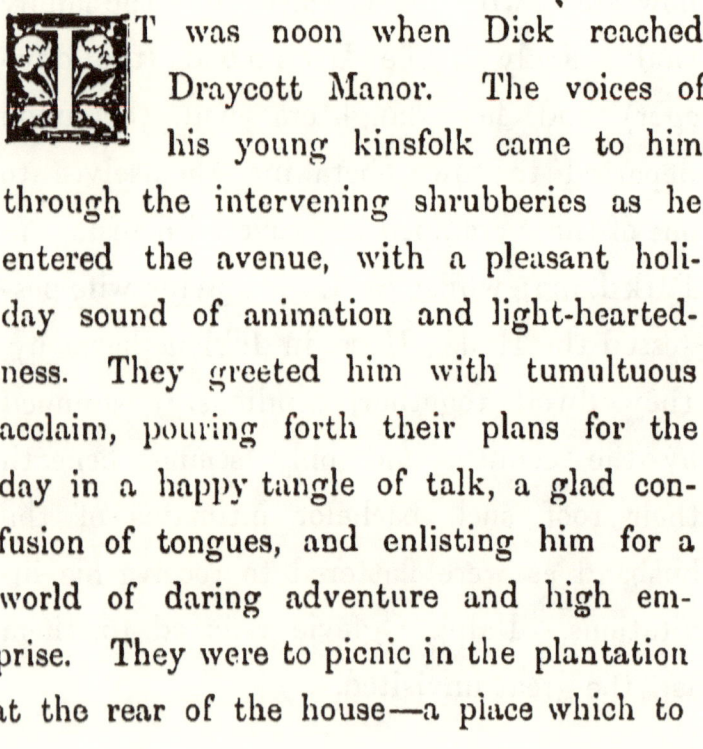

IT was noon when Dick reached Draycott Manor. The voices of his young kinsfolk came to him through the intervening shrubberies as he entered the avenue, with a pleasant holiday sound of animation and light-heartedness. They greeted him with tumultuous acclaim, pouring forth their plans for the day in a happy tangle of talk, a glad confusion of tongues, and enlisting him for a world of daring adventure and high emprise. They were to picnic in the plantation at the rear of the house—a place which to

Ethel (a young lady of liberal imagination, with a lively faith in the Jabberwock) was the veritable "tulgey wood" wherein Mr. Carroll's famous hybrid wontedly disported itself. They were to play at Indians, said little Sydney, impressively; and at Grizzly Bears; and at the Swiss Family Robinson, and the Arctic Crusoes—for the character of their outdoor games was mainly controlled by the course of Master Tom's study of fiction, whence his brother and sisters would one day find themselves called upon to enact the part of Delaware "braves" or treacherous Crows, and the next to undergo the hardships of desert island castaways and the like. Which exclusively masculine line of impersonation was the source of secret grievance to Dora and Ethel, who liefer would have represented their favourite heroines from Miss Edgeworth's pleasing tales, or the "Heir of Redcliffe," and the "Daisy Chain." Indeed,

so strong was this feeling in them at times,
that (with Viola or Rosalind, in man's attire)
they occasionally were fain to "play the
woman ;" and Tom, to his disgust, would not
unfrequently surprise his dreaded enemies,
War Eagle and Black Snake, talking together
like a couple of Miss Yonge's schoolgirls.
Wherefore the warrior's soul grew dark
within him, and the words of his tongue were
bitter as bruised laurels.

Having bestowed his birthday presents—
an illustrated edition of Hans Andersen for
Dora, and a pocket-knife of many blades and
ingenious accessories for Tom—Dick entered
the house to pay his respects to his godfather,
promising the children to join them in the
plantation as soon as possible. He found
Sydney Draycott, in silken dressing-gown
and slippers, smoking a mild-breathed cigarette, and conning his latest importation from
Paris—a sweet thing called *La Femme de*

Feu, one of those exquisite works of art which the capital of civilisation alone can produce us.

"Ah, my dear Richard! is that you?" quoth Mr. Draycott, extending a delicately smooth hand, to be taken—and shaken. " I hope you—er—are well. I understood you had come home (last week, was it not?), after your eccentric disappearance. Your mother mentioned it. Well, well! I was wild myself as a young man, and went through much the same kind of—er—thing. But it's a mistake, my dear boy; it's a mistake !"

Dick coloured, and said :

" I don't exactly understand, sir."

" Why, that sort of *liaison*. I speak to you, Richard, as one man of the world to another. Woman—lovely but illiterate woman—will inevitably pall upon a person of taste and education. I assure you I was—er —was infatuated, positively infatuated, with a young creature in Brussels once! The divine passion overcame me, and I—er—I sacrificed myself to it. But what was the result? In less than six weeks Lizette the smiling was Lizette the sulking! Her ignorance shocked me; her want of—er—of delicacy pained me to the heart. I was disappointed, disillusionised. My feeling was that of the young fellow in—er—in "Locksley Hall:"

> "'*I* to herd with narrow foreheads,
> *I* to mix with shallow brains!'

And so we—er—we parted. But there! you've learnt what it all is for yourself, no doubt."

"I beg your pardon!" broke in Dick, hotly. "I've learnt nothing like it! I suppose, sir, you are referring to that—that infernal lie about Phœbe Langham, the girl at Abingdon; and I'm very sorry you should seem to credit it."

"*Tiens, tiens!* My good young man, you —er—you excite yourself. And it isn't necessary. *Tout au contraire.* I—er—I do not blame you ; I am not reproaching you. There is nothing narrow, nothing illiberal, puritanical, about *me.* Far from it. Human frailty will ever find indulgence in *my* eyes. Others, my dear Richard, may censure you— may—er—may cast stones, so to speak—but your godfather will be lenient to the last; will be, in fact, always as you see him now. Let me offer you a cigarette ?"

Dick declined, bluntly stating that he preferred a pipe out-of-doors. Mr. Draycott resumed, with undiminished complacency :

" It's very nice in you to—er—to come and see me, Richard—very so. Since Dale has been in town, the only human being who's called on me is that—er—that old woman, Mrs. Towle—if, indeed, an old woman *is* a human being, as—er—as someone has doubted.

And she merely came for a subscription. But *à propos* of Dale, I—er—I hear he's likely to remain away some time. I—er—I understand he has fallen in with his old friend Ely, Sir Oliver Ely. African Ely, they call him at—er—at the Travellers'."

"Mr. Dale sent me a letter yesterday," said Dick. "He spoke about his friend Sir Oliver, but he made no mention of coming back to Idlewild yet."

"Just so, just so. *Ça se comprend.* Oglevie tells me he intends letting his—er—his daughter go to her aunt this season—to Mrs. Beresford Earl—and so, you see, the inducement with our dear friend Dale is to—er—to stay in town rather than return to the country."

"But I *don't* see!" ejaculated Dick, feeling, nevertheless, shaken by a sudden direful misgiving.

"No? Ah, true, true! I—er—I forgot

you had been away from us, and might not
have heard that Dale was—er—was *épris de
la belle Marguerite.*"

"A pree?" echoed Dick, blankly.

"Precisely! *Epris.* That I imagine to
be the—er—the Parisian equivalent for what
in London you would call ' awful spoons;' but
my English is somewhat behind-hand, somewhat behind-hand. Mrs. Towle (an objection-
able woman, dear boy, so—er—so coarse !)
asserts that Miss Oglevie has been aiming
at our friend from—er—from the beginning."

"That's false, I'll *swear!*" cried Dick, fire
in his eyes.

"Well, yes. I myself conceive it to be
placing the—er—the cart before the horse.
I mentioned the insinuation to Mr. Eliot—to
your father, in fact—and he remarked that
Mrs. Towle was one who would suspect Shakspere of going to—er—to Lamb's 'Tales '

for interested motives. Your father, Richard, has a—er—has a way of putting things which is somewhat happy, somewhat happy."

At this point there was a sound of wheels upon the drive near the house, and Sydney Draycott rose from his seat.

" Bless my soul! Why, that must be the Oglevies! Do you—er—do you mind just meeting them, whilst I make my *toilette?* You know the ways of the house, and—er— and so forth, and so forth. Thanks—a thousand!"

With this Mr. Draycott disappeared, and Dick went into the hall to receive the visitors. The suggestion of a possible attachment between Margaret Oglevie and Oscar Dale had confounded him, and he felt his heart burning with a bitter sense of the cruelty of fate, aggravated by an unreasoning protest against the misplaced affection of individuals. What! was all the love that had gathered and grown

within him to avail nothing ? the fond dreams
he had dreamt, the fair hopes he had cherished,
to come to nought ? Hitherto these sweet
imaginings of his had been vague as moonlit
mist upon a southern sea ; but now suddenly,
at a touch from without, they seemed to take
form and shape, and revealed him, sharply and
prophetically, how grievous, how utter and
intolerable, would be the loss he was
threatened with. How should he hold to the
good, how climb to the higher, if the hope
that inspired him were thus made hopeless—
if the hand that beckoned him might never
be clasped in his ? Dick knew his own weakness, his own urgent need ; and his heart
cried aloud—blindly, passionately—for the
help without which there would be stumbling
and falling and wandering away into darkness.

Such thoughts surged through Dick's mind
in the score or so seconds it took him to

traverse the hall and gain the outer door. Even as he opened it came a bright flash of comfort and relief. The whole story, perhaps, was baseless! Mrs. Towle? Mrs. Towle was an unscrupulous scandal-monger, a false prophet, and the truth was not in her. What a young fool he must be, to flurry himself for nothing! Mrs. Towle? Hang Mrs. Towle!

And he flung wide open the door, with a smile upon his face.

CHAPTER XV.

MARGARET AND DICK.

ARGARET OGLEVIE was just stepping from the carriage as Dick came forward to greet her.

She was not, perhaps, a beautiful girl in the ordinary acceptance of the term, which implies regularity of feature, a rosebud mouth, and a complexion of strawberries and cream; but in her face was that higher beauty of expression, that rarer and more eloquent beauty of soul, which made her seem, beside the conventional model, as the Rhodian girl Balaustion might seem beside a portrait of Sir Peter Lely's. Our education is not enough advanced to permit us to describe her dress, or even to name the materials composing it ; we can only say that it was black, relieved with white.

Now, we have seen studies in black and white which were hard, graceless, aggressive —things to set the teeth on edge, and make one conscious of one's spinal marrow ; and we have seen others that were soft, harmonious, and altogether precious. There is a black and white as commonplace as print and paper, as crude as an auctioneer's hand-bill ; and there is a black and white as poetical as summer midnight and sea-foam. Margaret Oglevie had a perception of the true significance of dress which is the gift of but few women among us, and could no more assume an inharmonious colour than she could use a coarse expression or utter a falsehood. As she stood before Richard Eliot in her simple grace of girlhood, the

sunlight falling on her sweet pale face and
earnest eyes, she seemed to his fancy such
stuff as angels are made of, and there rose
in his heart a feeling which was a wordless
prayer.

"Well, young man!" said Mr. Oglevie,
nodding to Dick, "and where's godpapa?"

Dick tendered his explanation, and led the
way into the house.

"I'm so glad you've come to the children
to-day," said Margaret, lingering at the
threshold of the library, which her father
had entered. "I thought you would; I
know they expected you. Papa has a whole
afternoon's business to do with Mr. Draycott,
who is joint trustee in that Jermyn estate,
I believe; and, as Miss Jane is still away,
why, I'm free to fish, or picnic, or play
Robinson Crusoe, or do anything the children like. Where are they all?"

"They are in the plantation," answered

Dick. "As soon as Mr. Draycott comes we'll contrive to get off and join them. Will you?"

"Yes, sir, I will. By-the-by, we've got presents for Dora and Tom in the carriage; but I'll leave them till we return. I've also brought something for the other three, as I fancy small children are apt to think a brother's or sister's birthday rather a poor and partial affair if it doesn't result in gifts all round. *I* should, I'm sure."

Presently Mr. Draycott appeared, and the two young people were thereupon dismissed by Mr. Oglevie as superfluous. They accordingly set off for the plantation.

"I wanted to see you," began Margaret, in her low, clear voice, breaking the silence that had held them whilst yet within the Manor gardens. "I have read the poems you let me have, and I wished to thank you, and tell you how much I like them."

Dick looked up eagerly, with kindling eye and cheek ; there was more concerned than merely an author's vanity. After a minute's pause, Margaret resumed.

" But they are too *triste,* I think. There's a sort of mist of melancholy hanging over them that seems to me to make their atmosphere hardly a healthy one. And they are so uninhabited."

" Uninhabited ?"

" I mean, they have so little humanity. They are like those beautiful desert islands one reads of—full of flowers, and rare colour, and dreamy woods—where the wind sighs and the sound of the waves is heard, but with no faces of men and women to come and meet you when you land. You see I dare to criticise."

" Please go on ; tell me just what you think."

" Well, then, they are almost all retro-

spective.   Now, that ought not to be.
Here's one, for instance" (and Margaret
drew a roll of manuscript from the small
bag, with quaint silver clasp and chasing,
that hung from her girdle). "Just let me
read out the first two verses of this.
May I ?"

Dick nodded, and Margaret began—

"'O the wild days of youth, the dear dead days !
    Dark are the lights and all the chorus dumb,
And cold and faintly through the gath'ring haze
    Of this sad twilight time thin echoes come,
And wand'ring voices haunt the glimmering ways.

"'Sitting alone in these last empty years,
    Life, starved and dwindled, tells its old tales o'er,
And, like a wind, the Past sings in my ears,
    And, like a wind, goes by. Alas! no more
For me the glad green spring of smiles and tears!'"

Now pray what do you mean by that?   If
you were three score years and ten, I could
understand it ; but at your time of life you
—well !   I was going to say you are young
enough to know better ; but at least you
ought to write otherwise."

"I suppose I wrote as I felt at the time," said Dick, with a half sigh, "and that wasn't very lively. It was whilst I was living in Soho, and the look-out over London seemed wofully ugly and bare, and brick-and-mortary—full of imperfect creations and half-built designs. And so, you see," concluded he, with a touch of his father's quickness, "I preferred the ruins of the past to the scaffold-poles of the present."

"Scaffold-poles may not be very lovely or picturesque," said Margaret, "but at least they carry with them a promise, and indicate a future."

"And also a past," added Dick; "they were once trees! I always feel sorry for scaffold-poles!"

"I don't," cried Margaret, a little wilfully. "And if they are good scaffold-poles, I dare say they are glad to help to build houses, and to be of use in the world."

"Pleased to think, perhaps," said Dick,
"'that men may rise on stepping-stones of
their dead selves to higher things.' You
mean that, I suppose?"

"Yes, I mean that. But we are running
away from our subject, which is your poems,
recollect. They were not *all* written in
Soho, were they? Take any other—this
about autumn—

> 'What time fair Autumn, musing, walked abroad—
> She of the dreamy eye and bounteous breast,
> And lip fruit-stain'd, and calm brow loosely tress'd,
> Her paths'——

But I shan't finish it, because it gets dreary,
and dolorous, and hopeless, and morbid.
Morbid! That was the word I wanted!"

"I thank thee for that word," interjected
Dick, a little ruefully. Then, in a changed
tone—

"Why don't you yourself write? You
who are—who are so far, far better and
wiser than I!"

Something in Dick's voice made Margaret's heart give a little leap, and she felt a sudden vague timidness come over her. But she answered quickly—

"Wiser and better! Suppose, just for argument's sake, I *am* wise and good; what has that to do with writing poetry? Dr. Johnson was wise, and Dr. Watts was good; but a song of Burns' is worth all the verses they ever penned, or could have penned!"

"But you do write sometimes, don't you?"

"Oh! yes," replied Margaret, lightly. "'Thoughts that breathe and words that burn'—in my bedroom fireplace."

"But seriously?"

"Seriously, then—no, not now. A year ago I used to write a terrible amount, but lately I've grown afraid. I think papa's styling my pieces 'effusions' had something to do with it. If I can't produce a poem, I'll

never again be guilty of an effusion! You
know what Aurora Leigh says :

> ' I had rather dance
> At fairs on tight-rope, till the babies dropt
> Their gingerbread for joy, than shift the type
> For tolerable verse— *intolerable*
> To men who act and suffer !' "

Dick chose to feel this as a rebuke to
himself, and vindictively slashed with his
stick at the heads of a group of tall thistles,
which stood like sentinels at the entry of the
plantation. Margaret intuitively divined his
thoughts.

"Of course," she said, hastily, "I am
speaking simply of myself and my own personal feelings about verse-writing. As to
you, I envy you most wickedly. I think
your poems——"

And she straightway said what she thought
of Dick Eliot's rhymings, paying him many
delicate compliments, and speaking of them

with at least the average impartiality of a
woman when criticising a man in whose
favour she is predisposed. But probably no
author was ever *quite* satisfied with the
opinion he has sought and elicited, however
flattering such opinion may be. We cannot,
perhaps, see ourselves as others see us ; but
then neither can others see us as we see ourselves. They miss our subtlest points, and
seldom fully realise how charming is our
divine philosophy. Quoth a dear friend, to
whose judgment we submitted the manuscript of the present novel, " Its tone is
such-and-such, and its tendency so-and-so ;"
whereupon we said with severity, " Cassio,
we love thee ; but never more be counsellor
of ours." Which showed a dignified and
proper spirit under incompetent criticism.

Before Margaret Oglevie had finished con-
veying to Dick her sentiments regarding his
compositions, their approach was detected by

the party of little Draycotts, and immediately a rush of five put an end to the *tête-à-tête.* It was pleasant to see how the children all gathered round Margaret; how, as she bent down to kiss them, she whispered a word in the ear of each of the mysterious "something" she had brought for them from Norwich; and how, hearing which, their bright eyes grew brighter with a delightful sense of secrecy and anticipation. What had they been doing? asked Margaret; and what were they going to do? They had played at Indians, of course. (Tom was hot on the track of the Redskin just at this time, having obtained an early introduction to Mayne Reid)—and had built a wigwam, and laid an ambush (into which Ethel had obligingly fallen), and finally had smoked the pipe of peace—a real pipe, borrowed from Hobbs, the gardener, the bowl whereof Tom had loaded with lighted

brown paper, causing that venerable chief
Grey Beaver (little Sydney) to choke to
such an extent that the council was abruptly
broken up.

And now they wanted to play at amphi-
theatres, and gladiators, and early Christian
martyrs ("In the reign of Diocletian," put
in Dora, glibly); and would Miss Oglevie be
a noble Roman lady, and be sure and turn
her thumb down when she wished Tom to
make an end of Ethel? And they had got
old Rough, the yard-dog, for one of the
"beasts" the Christians used to fight with,
said Tom (whose predilection for the Christians was obviously based on an exaggerated
idea of their pugnacity); and he had brought
a net off a cherry-tree from the back-garden
wall, in order, it appeared, to renew (with
Dora) the old classical contest of net and
trident against sword and shield.

Margaret Oglevie was immensely amused

at all this, and entered into it *con amore.*
The proposed scenes in the arena were, it
seemed, the outgrowth of sundry lessons in
Roman history which their governess, Miss
Beckett (Lydia Brooke's successor) had
recently given them, combined with the
study of an engraving of Gerome's "Pollice
Verso!" in the possession of their father.
The history of Rome had, indeed, attracted
them from the first, since Miss Beckett,
starting *ab ovo*, had begun by introducing
them to Romulus and Remus, the simple
fact of whose twinship naturally ingratiated
them with Dora and Tom ; albeit the former
(in confidence to Ethel) never ceased to regret
that Remus wasn't a girl.

The April hours passed brightly and
swiftly. It was a happy afternoon, and
Dick long remembered it. For him it was
joy enough to be beside Margaret, to watch
her eyes gladden with the gladness about

her, and to see the soft colour, tender as the
outer petals of the dogrose, gather in her
cheek beneath the spring wind's breezy
caresses. Sorrow and sickness and death—
this is the earth's inheritance; but, despite
these three, come youth and love and spring,
from generation to generation renewing their
sweet promise, and filling the lands with
fragrance. For God loves the earth, remembering it is the work of His hand, and
year after year gives it these good gifts to
make it beautiful and pleasing in the sight
of Heaven.

Returning home to the Manor, the children, flushed and flower-laden, wandered
away in advance of their two seniors; save
Baby Draycott, whom Dick carried on his
arm, her tired little head drooping upon his
shoulder, and her little hand gradually re-
laxing its hold of the buttercups (spoils of
gold!) she had gathered.

"Ah, what a pleasant time we've had!" said Margaret. "And next week I shall be leaving all the green fields and the woods and flowers behind me!"

"It's true, then?" exclaimed Dick. "You are really going to London? Mr. Draycott spoke of it this morning."

"Yes, it's true. My aunt has long been wanting me to come, and now, at last, I'm going. I don't like leaving papa at home alone; but he has promised me to run up as often as he can. You, too, will be in town next month, won't you?"

"I think—I hope so. You know I dare to dream of literature as a profession; and, if only I can settle in London, Oscar Dale offers me a host of introductions. I do so want to go!—I care for nothing else! With Dale away, and you as well, it would be dreary work hanging about here all the summer by myself."

There was silence between them for a minute or two. The thoughts of each had taken flight into the dim debateable land of possibilities. Dick Eliot, conscious of powers quickening within him, whereof even his nearest scarce had suspicion, imagined a future fair and roseate, satisfactory as day-break to a night-watcher. And the crown of it all was a smile upon a girl's face, a word from a girl's lips!

Margaret's fancies were hardly so sanguine. Before her rose the vision of a man grown tired and impatient, sick at heart with hope deferred, ill-nourished with faint praise. And this man would need sympathy and encouragement, and the touch of a friend's hand. A fount of tenderness welled up in her breast, craving—passionately and im-peratively—some womanly manifestation, some characteristic outlet in present action.

"Let me take the child," said she; and

Dick, recalled from the man's confident
dream of triumph and masterful achievement, looked at her in momentary surprise,
not comprehending the faltering of her
voice.

"She's heavy for you, I'm sure. Please
let me take her," petitioned Margaret. "I
wish it."

Dick gently complied. The warm, unconscious little burden was shifted from his
arms to Margaret's, against whose bosom it
nestled lovingly. It was a pretty picture
they made, as the girl took the child from
the young man, and they stood together in
the green wood bending over it, while the
western sky grew tender. Around them
the spring leaves whispered and the birds
sang, and the pulse of the young year beat
gladly. Nature seemed conspiring with
their hearts to draw them nearer one to
another. An exquisite harmony, born of

mingled sound and silence, pervaded all,
blending the lisp of April foliage and the
thrush's evensong with the wide calm of
colour that flooded the West, and filling
their souls to overflowing.

Dick stayed dinner at the Manor, and
spent the evening with Mr. Draycott and
his guests. After Margaret Oglevie and
her father had departed, he set off in the
moonlight for his walk home across the
fields. His heart was full of tenderness,
his brain teeming with warm poetic fancies
and glowing aspirations and high resolves.
When he reached his own bedroom he flung
open the casement, and leant out of the
window, breathing the cool sweetness of the
dewy garden below, and listening to the
persistent cry of the corncrake from distant
meadows. In his hand was a vignette portrait which Margaret had that day given
him—a photograph of herself long promised.

Girls nowadays hand these trifles to men when asked, much as they pass the mustard to their neighbour at table ; but not quite so lightly had this one been sought and bestowed. Dick looked long and earnestly at the face it pictured ere putting it away among the dearer-cherished treasures of his desk. And before thus resigning it, he had written in pencil on the back these four lines :

> " *Pale is my love, than ever lily purer,*
> *Sweeter she is than roses after rain ;*
> *And, for my faith, I cannot need a surer*
> *Than in her grace, that maketh God's grace plain.*"

END OF VOL. II.

BILLING AND SONS, PRINTERS, GUILDFORD, SURREY

APRIL, 1878.

SAMUEL TINSLEY & CO.'S

PUBLICATIONS.

London:

SAMUEL TINSLEY & CO.,

10, SOUTHAMPTON STREET, STRAND.

₊ *Totally distinct from any other firm of Publishers.*

NOTICE.

Any books in this List will be sent post-free on receipt of the published price, or may be ordered through any Bookseller.

*** ALL COMMUNICATIONS AND MANUSCRIPTS SHOULD BE DISTINCTLY ADDRESSED TO MESSRS. SAMUEL TINSLEY AND CO., 10, SOUTHAMPTON STREET, STRAND, LONDON, W.C., AND WILL RECEIVE PROMPT ATTENTION.

APRIL 10, 1878.

10, SOUTHAMPTON STREET, STRAND.

SAMUEL TINSLEY & CO.'S
NEW PUBLICATIONS.

——∞⦂⚙⦂∞——

POPULAR NEW THREE-VOLUME NOVELS.

HE LITTLE LOO : a Tale of the South Sea. By SYDNEY MOSTYN, author of "The Surgeon's Secret," &c. 3 vols., 31s. 6d.

" Mr. Mostyn's story is full of thrilling interest from the first page to the last. It is capitally written, with an obviously intimate knowledge of the minutiæ of the merchant service, and of seamen's habits and methods of life. Some of the descriptive passages—for instance, the account of the storm by which the vessel was assailed shortly before the mutiny—are full of vigour and realism. . . . . Altogether, this story of the sea is one of the best books of its kind that has appeared of late years."—*Scotsman.*

THRO' THE SHADOW. 2 vols., 21s.

LOVE LOST, BUT HONOUR WON. By THEO-DORE RUSSELL MONRO, author of " The Vandeleurs of Red Tor." 3 vols., 31s. 6d.

" It is readable and fairly interesting."—*Standard.*

" The tale is told with a vigour and dash of style which are enjoyable : and the plot, improbable though it be, is developed with much skill."—*Scotsman.*

" Mr. Monro, in his latest novel, shows that his powers as a writer of fiction are of no mean order. The plot is well constructed, and evolved without any startling violation of the probabilities, whilst, although its nature is tolerably obvious from the beginning, the reader is kept in a sufficient amount of uncertainty as to how matters will end to prevent any loss of interest. Added to which there appears considerable talent for the delineation of character. . . . . A story which raises the happiest auguries for Mr. Monro's future as a novelist, and which can hardly fail to obtain success."—*Morning Post.*

SALTHURST: a Novel. By Mrs. ARTHUR LEWIS, author of " The Master of Riverswood." 3 vols., 31s. 6d.

" Exhibits, in respect of literary quality, dramatic power, and truth and vigour in the conception and creation of character, a distinct advance on her former work, 'The Master of Riverswood,' which was itself a powerful and well-written' tale. . . . . There is a freshness and a sense of living emotion pervading it all through. . . . . Some of the minor personages, as well as the principal characters, are very happily drawn, with a kind of tender simplicity which gives realistic effects such as no amount of elaboration could attain."—*Scotsman.*

LAWRENCE LOFTEWALDE. By ARTHUR HAMILTON. 3 vols., 31s. 6d.

Samuel Tinsley & Co, 10, Southampton St., Strand.

THE LAST OF THE HADDONS. By Mrs.
NEWMAN, author of "Too Late," &c.   3 vols., 31s. 6d.

"A very touching story."— *Standard*.

"The story is well told, and the characters of Mary, Philip, and Lilian are all such as to excite the interest of the reader."—*Scotsman*.

"Extremely interesting—the heroine writes to a high standard of unselfishness, yet somehow her self-denial never seems unnatural. All the characters are well drawn—none of them are hackneyed. The distinction between conventional and true vulgarity is skilfully illustrated. The book is throughout pure, refined, and amusing."—*Athenæum*.

"A good and interesting story, having vigorous, well-drawn characters, and being told in language at once simple and forcible."—*John Bull*.

"The whole story has a sort of idyllic flavour about it, which is quite charming."—*Sunday Times*.

COUSIN DEBORAH'S WHIM: a Novel. By MARY
E. SHIPLEY, author of "Gabrielle Vaughan," &c.   3 vols., 31s. 6d.

"A good deal can be said in favour of 'Cousin Deborah's Whim.' The tone is fairly wholesome, the style good, and the fiction well thought out. . . . . The authoress has devoted much thought to the delineation of her heroine's disposition. The attempt alone is sufficient to earn a good word from all who see in character-drawing the highest type of fiction ; and Miss Shipley has done something more than attempt to succeed."—*Athenæum*.

"There is a great deal of thought and careful literary workmanship in 'Cousin Deborah's Whim.' . . . . It is a patient, elaborate, and, on the whole, a truthful study of two very opposite types of character, and of the way in which each is affected by mutual contact and external circumstances. . . . The story is pleasantly written, and not only the two principal figures but many of the minor personages are depicted with much insight and realism."—*Scotsman*.

POPULAR NEW NOVELS, &c., each complete in One Volume.

HE REIGN OF ROSAS; or, South American Sketches. By E. C. FERNAU. Cr. 8vo., 7s. 6d.

"It is this tyranny which the author has undertaken to illustrate in her very pleasant and interesting book. . . . The lively portraiture of Argentine life and manners amply relieves the more gloomy sketches.'—*Academy*.

"All are replete with graphic sketches of the country, its customs and society in 'camp' and city, which exhibit enviable powers of observation and description. . . . These charming South American sketches cannot fail to interest the general reader ; while to those who are familiar with her scenes, and have seen her remarkable characters in the flesh, there is an associating link of irresistible attraction."—*Coming Events*.

"'Dolores' is the most tragic and impressive, yet at the same time unpretending, story we have read for a long time."—*Hornet*.

THE EARL OF EFFINGHAM. By LALLA
M'DOWELL, author of "How we Learned to Help Ourselves." Crown 8vo., 7s. 6d.

REGENT ROSALIND : a Story.   By the author
of "Workaday Briars," &c.   Crown 8vo., 7s. 6d.

"'Regent Rosalind' shows much better than any discourse how a sensible and motherly girl can line again the shattered nest of her home."—
Miss Yonge in *Womankind*.

"The story is a pleasant and readable one, containing some truthful
pictures of life in a great English provincial town, and several thoughtful
and finished studies of character. . . . The interest of the tale, though not
enthralling for readers who are accustomed to the highly spiced sensational
fiction of the day, is steadily maintained to the close, and is always healthy
and natural."—*Scotsman*.

"It is to be hoped that there exist even now a certain number of young
persons whose taste is sufficiently unvitiated to permit them to read this
simple story—written in unusually good English ; and which deals with
nothing out of the way of the homely life of thousands of English middle-
class homes—with appreciation and interest. . . . The author of ' Regent
Rosalind' has drawn a bright, honest, lovable, pleasant girl's portrait for
us, and the accessories are all natural and well developed. . . . We have
read ' Regent Rosalind' with a sense of restful pleasure."—*Spectator*.

A SUSSEX IDYL.   By CLEMENTINA BLACK
Crown 8vo., 7s. 6d.

"'A Sussex Idyl' is thoroughly deserving of its name—no mean praise,
as it seems to us. For what is more difficult in these feverish modern
times than to produce a true idyl—an idyl of to-day, not thrown back into
the quiet centuries that lie behind us, but true and living, even as the lanes
and meadows and bird-haunted copses are still true and living ? . . . 'A
Sussex Idyl' is such a charming story that we should indeed be ungratefu.
did we not look forward with pleasure to more work from the same hand.'
—*Examiner*.

"There is a good deal to like in ' A Sussex Idyl.' It is in every way
what its title implies, for the story has much freshness and grace, and its
pictures have a distinct local colouring and a fidelity to nature, which may
be appreciated even by those who have never spent a day in a Sussex hop-
garden. . . . 'A Sussex Idyl' may be welcomed as highly promising."—
Athenæum.

IN TROPIC SEAS : a Tale of the Spanish Main.
By W. WESTALL, author of " Tales and Legends of Saxony
and Lusatia."   Crown 8vo., 7s. 6d.

IN THE SPRING OF MY LIFE : a Love Story.
By the Princess OLGA CANTACUZÈNE. (From the French.)
Crown 8vo., 7s. 6d.

MILES : a Town Story.   By the author of " Fan."
Crown 8vo., 5s.

SIR AUBYN'S HOUSEHOLD.   By SIGMA.
Author of " Fan."   Crown 8vo., 7s. 6d.

TEN TIMES PAID : a Story.   By BRUTON
BLOSSE. Crown 8vo., 7s. 6d.

SOPHIA : a Novel. By JANE ASHTON. Crown
8vo., price 7s. 6d.

LOVED AND UNLOVED : a Story. By HARRIET
DAVIS. Crown 8vo., 7s. 6d.

Samuel Tinsley & Co., 10, Southampton St., Strand.

IN THE PRESS.

THE LIFE AND ADVENTURES OF AN UN-
FORTUNATE AUTHOR. Written by HIMSELF.
Crown 8vo., 7s. 6d.

GEORGE HERN: a Novel. By HENRY GLEMHAM.
3 vols., price 31s. 6d.

FRANK ALLERTON : an Autobiography.   By
AUGUSTUS MONGREDIEN. 3 vols. 31s. 6d.

ELIOT THE YOUNGER : a Fiction in Freehand.
By BERNARD BARKER.   3 vols. 31s. 6d.

LADY'S HOLM. By ANNIE L. WALKER, author of
"Against Her Will," "A Canadian Heroine," &c. 3 vols. 31s.6d.

THE FAIR MAID OF TAUNTON : a Tale of
the Siege. By ELIZABETH M. ALFORD. Crown 8vo., 6s.

UNTO WHICH SHE WAS NOT BORN. By
ELLEN GADESDEN. Crown 8vo., 7s. 6d.
"A trouble weighed upon her and perplexed her night and morn,
With the burden of an honour unto which she was not born."
TENNYSON.

RIVERSDALE COURT. By MRS. FORREST
GRANT, author of " Fair, but not Wise, &c. 3 vols. 31s. 6d.

SKETCHES IN CORNWALL. By M. F. BRAGGE.
In Wrapper, price 1s.

CHRISTIERN THE WICKED: an Historical
Tale. By H. S. TAGSON. (The Author's Translation.)
Crown 8vo., 7s. 6d.

THE GREGORS: a Cornish Story. By JANE H.
SPETTIGUE. Crown 8vo., 7s. 6d.

SAMUEL TINSLEY & CO.'S
PUBLICATIONS.

THE POPULAR NOVELS, AT ALL LIBRARIES IN TOWN AND COUNTRY.

AGAINST HER WILL. By ANNIE L. WALKER, Author of "A Canadian Heroine." 3 vols., 31s. 6d.

The **Spectator** says :—"Altogether 'Against her Will' is a clever, wholesome novel, which we can recommend without reservation."

The **Standard** says :—" 'Against her Will' is a very powerful novel, and one which we can on every account recommend to our readers."

The **Graphic** says :—"The book is full of good and careful work from end to end, and very much above the average level of merit."

The **Scotsman** says :—" 'Against her Will' is a novel of sterling merit."

ALDEN OF ALDENHOLME. By GEORGE SMITH. 3 vols., 31s. 6d.

ALICE GODOLPHIN and A LITTLE HEIRESS. By MARY NEVILLE. In 2 vols., 21s.

ALL ROUND THE WORLD; or, What's the Object? By FRANK FOSTER, author of "Number One ; or, The Way of the World," etc., etc. 3 vols., 31s. 6d.

AS THE SHADOWS FALL: a Novel. By J. EDWARD MUDDOCK, author of "A Wingless Angel," etc. 3 vols., 31s. 6d.

ANNALS of the TWENTY-NINTH CENTURY : or, the Autobiography of the Tenth President of the World-Republic. 3 vols., 31s. 6d.

" Here is a work in certain respects one of the most singular in modern literature, which surpasses all of its class in bold and luxuriant imagination, in vivid descriptive power, in startling—not to say extravagant suggestions

---

Samuel Tinsley & Co., 10, Southampton St., Strand.

—in lofty and delicate moral sympathies. . . . . We have read his work with almost equal feelings of pleasure, wonderment, and amusement, and this, we think, will be the feelings of most of its readers. On the whole, it is a book of remarkable novelty, and unquestionable genius."—*Nonconformist.*

ARE YOU MY WIFE? By GRACE RAMSAY, author of "Iza's Story," "A Woman's Trials," etc. 3 vols., 31s. 6d.

BARBARA'S WARNING. By the author of "Recommended to Mercy." 3 vols., 31s. 6d.

BARONET'S CROSS, THE. By MARY MEEKE, author of "Marion's Path through Shadow to Sunshine." 2 vols., 21s.

BETWEEN TWO LOVES. By ROBERT J. GRIFFITHS, LL.D. 3 vols., 31s. 6d.

BITTER to SWEET END. By E. HOSKEN. 3 vols., 31s. 6d.

"A pleasant taking story, full of interest, and entirely unobjectionable."—*Literary Churchman.*

"There is a genuine tone of humour about much of the conversation, and a natural bearing about the heroine which give very pleasant reading, and a good deal of interest and amusement to the book. . . . . On the whole we cannot but praise 'Bitter to Sweet End.'"—*Public Opinion.*

BLUEBELL. By Mrs. G. C. HUDDLESTON. 3 vols., 31s. 6d.

"Sparkling, well-written, spirited, and may be read with certainty of amusement."—*Sunday Times.*

BRANDON TOWER. A Story. 3 vols., 31s. 6d.

"Familiar matter of to-day."

CHASTE AS ICE, PURE AS SNOW. By Mrs. M. C. DESPARD. 3 vols., 31s. 6d. Second Edition.

"A novel of something more than ordinary promise."—*Graphic.*

CLAUDE HAMBRO. By JOHN C. WESTWOOD. 3 vols., 31s. 6d.

COUSIN DEBORAH'S WHIM. A Novel; By MARY E. SHIPLEY, author of "Gabrielle Vaughan," etc. 3 vols., 31s. 6d.

CRUEL CONSTANCY. By KATHARINE KING, author of "The Queen of the Regiment." 3 vols., 31s. 6d.

DAYS OF HIS VANITY, THE. By SYDNEY GRUNDY. 3 vols., 31s. 6d.

DESPERATE CHARACTER, A : A Tale of the Gold Fever. By W. THOMSON-GREGG. 3 vols., 31s. 6d.
"A novel which cannot fail to interest."—*Daily News.*

D'EYNCOURTS OF FAIRLEIGH, THE. By THOMAS ROWLAND SKEMP. 3 vols., 31s. 6d.

DONE IN THE DARK. By the author of "Recommended to Mercy." 3 vols., 31s. 6d.

DR. MIDDLETON'S DAUGHTER. By the author of "A Desperate Character." 3 vols., 31s. 6d.

DULCIE. By LOIS LUDLOW. 3 vols., 31s. 6d.

ELIOT THE YOUNGER : a Fiction in Freehand. By BERNARD BARKER. 3 vols., 31s. 6d.

FAIR, BUT NOT FALSE. By EVELYN CAMPBELL. 3 vols., 31s. 6d.

FAIR, BUT NOT WISE. By Mrs. FORREST-GRANT. 2 vols., 21s.

FAIR IN THE FEARLESS OLD FASHION. By CHARLES FARMLET. 2 vols., 21s.

FIRST AND LAST. By F. VERNON-WHITE. 2 vols., 21s.

FOLLATON PRIORY. 2 vols., 21s.

FRANK ALLERTON : an Autobiography. By AUGUSTUS MONGREDIEN. 3 vols., 31s. 6d.

FRANK AMOR. By JAJABEE. 3 vols., 31s. 6d.

GAUNT ABBEY. By ELIZABETH J. LYSAGHT, author of "Building upon Sand," "Nearer and Dearer," etc. 3 vols., 31s. 6d.

GEORGE HERN : a Novel. By HENRY GLEMHAM. 3 vols., 31s. 6d.

GERALD BOYNE. By T. W. EAMES. 3 vols., 31s. 6d.

GILMORY. By PHŒBE ALLEN. 3 vols., 31s. 6d.

GOLD DUST. A Story. 3 vols., 31s. 6d.

GOLDEN MEMOIRS. By EFFIE LEIGH. 2 vols., 21s.

GRANTHAM SECRETS. By PHŒBE M. FEILDEN. 3 vols., 31s. 6d.

GRAYWORTH: a Story of Country Life. By CAREY HAZELWOOD. 3 vols., 31s. 6d.

GREED'S LABOUR LOST. By the Author of "Recommended to Mercy," etc. 3 vols., 31s. 6d.

EIR OF REDDESMONT, THE. 3 vols., 31s. 6d.

HER GOOD NAME. By J. FORTREY BOUVERIE. 3 vols., 31s. 6d.

HER IDOL. By MAXWELL HOOD. 3 vols., 31s. 6d.

HILDA AND I. By MRS. HARTLEY. 2 vols., 21s.
"An interesting, well-written, and natural story."—*Public Opinion.*

HILLESDEN ON THE MOORS. By ROSA MAC-KENZIE KETTLE, Author of the Mistress of Langdale Hall." 2 vols., 21s.

HIS LITTLE COUSIN. By EMMA MARIA PEARSON, Author of "One Love in a Life." 3 vols., 31s. 6d.

HIS SECOND WIFE. By MRS. EILOART, Author of "Meg," "Just a Woman," "Woman's Wrong," etc. 3 vols. 31s. 6d.

HOUSE OF CLARISFORD, THE: a Novel. By FREDERICK WOODMAN. 3 vols. 31s. 6d.

N BONDS, BUT FETTERLESS: a Tale of Old Ulster. By RICHARD CUNNINGHAME. 2 vols., 21s.

IN SECRET PLACES. By ROBERT J. GRIFFITHS, LL.D. 3 vols., 31s. 6d.

IN SPITE OF FORTUNE. By MAURICE GAY. 3 vols., 31s. 6d.

IN TROPIC SEAS: a Tale of the Spanish Main. By W. WESTALL. Crown 8vo., 7s. 6d.

IS IT FOR EVER? By KATE MAINWARING. 3 vols., 31s. 6d.

JABEZ EBSLEIGH, M.P. By Mrs. EILOART, Author of " The Curate's Discipline," " Meg," " Kate Randal's Bargain," etc. 3 vols., 31s. 6d.

JESSIE OF BOULOGNE. By the Rev. C. GILL-MOR, M.A. 3 vols., 31s. 6d.

KATE BYRNE. By S. HOWARD TAYLOR. 2 vols., 21s.

KATE RANDAL'S BARGAIN. By Mrs. EILOART, Author of " The Curate's Discipline," " Some of Our Girls," " Meg," &c. 3 vols., 31s. 6d.

KITTY'S RIVAL. By SYDNEY MOSTYN, Author of " The Surgeon's Secret," etc. 3 vols., 31s. 6d.

LADY LOUISE. By KATHLEEN ISABELLE CLARGES. 3 vols., 31s. 6d.

LADY'S HOLM. By ANNIE L. WALKER, author of " Against Her Will," " A Canadian Heroine," &c. 3 vols. 31s. 6d.

LASCARE: a Tale. 3 vols., 31s. 6d.

LAST OF THE HADDONS, THE. By Mrs. NEW-MAN, Author of " Too Late," etc. 3 vols., 31s. 6d.

LAWRENCE LOFTEWALDE. By ARTHUR HAMILTON. 3 vols., 31s. 6d.

LIFE OUT OF DEATH: a Romance. 3 vols., 31s. 6d.

LITTLE LOO, THE: a Story of the South Sea. By SIDNEY MOSTYN. Author of " Kitty's Rival," " The Surgeon's Secret," &c. 3 vols. 31s. 6d.

LLANTHONY COCKLEWIG: an Autobiographical Sketch of His Life and Adventures. By the Rev. STEPHEN SHEPHERD MAGUTH, LL.B., Cantab. 3 vols., 31s. 6d.

LORD CASTLETON'S WARD. By Mrs. B. R. GREEN. 3 vols., 31s. 6d.

LOVE LOST, BUT HONOUR WON. By THEODORE RUSSELL MONRO, Author of " The Vandeleurs of Red Tor," etc. 3 vols., 31s. 6d.

LOVE THAT LIVED, The. By Mrs. Eiloart, Author of "The Curate's Discipline," "Just a Woman," "Woman's Wrong," &c. 3 vols., 31s. 6d.
"Three volumes which most people will prefer not to leave till they have read the last page of the third volume."—*Pall Mall Gazette.*
"One of the most thoroughly wholesome novels we have read for some time."—*Scotsman.*

MADAME. By Frank Lee Benedict, Author of "St. Simon's Niece," etc. 3 vols., 31s. 6d.

MAGIC OF LOVE, The. By Mrs. Forrest-Grant, Author of "Fair, but not Wise." 3 vols., 31s. 6d.
"A very amusing novel."—*Scotsman.*

MAID ELLICE. By Theo. Gift. Author of "Pretty Miss Bellew," &c. 3 vols., 31s. 6d.

MAR'S WHITE WITCH. By Gertrude Douglas, Author of "Brown as a Berry," etc. 3 vols., 31s. 6d.
"A thoroughly good novel, which we can cordially recommend to our readers. . . We should not have grudged a little extra length to the story ; . . . for 'Mar's White Witch' is one of those rare novels in which it is a cause of regret, rather than of satisfaction, to arrive at the end of the third volume."—*John Bull.*

MASTER OF RIVERSWOOD, The. By Mrs. Arthur Lewis. 3 vols., 31s. 6d.

MART AND MANSION : a Tale of Struggle and Rest. By Philip Massinger. 3 vols., 31s. 6d.

MARY GRAINGER : A Story. By George Leigh. 2 vols., 21s.

MR. VAUGHAN'S HEIR. By Frank Lee Benedict, Author of "Miss Dorothy's Charge," etc., 3 vols., 31s. 6d.

NAME'S WORTH, A. By Mrs. M. Allen. 2 vols., 21s.

NEARER AND DEARER. By Elizabeth J. Lysaght, Author of "Building upon Sand." 3 vols., 31s. 6d.

NO FATHERLAND. By Madame Von Oppen. 2 vols., 21s.

ONLY SEA AND SKY. By Elizabeth Hindley. 2 vols., 21s.

OVER THE FURZE. By ROSA M. KETTLE, Author of the " Mistress of Langdale Hall," etc. 3 vols., 31s. 6d.

PENELOPE'S WEB : a Story. By LOUIS WITHRED. 3 vols., 31s. 6d.

PERCY LOCKHART. By F. W. BAXTER. 2 vols., 21s.

RECTOR OF OXBURY, THE : a Novel. 3 vols., 31s. 6d.

"This is a very good novel, written throughout in a generous catholic spirit . . . The book is full of kindly humour, and we heartily recommend it to our readers."—*Standard.*

"No doubt the real hero of this history is not the Rector, but the Dissenting minister, whose sufferings at the hand of his congregation are so graphically depicted. . . . The change which comes over poor Philip Holland's feelings. . . . is drawn with considerable power and dramatic skill."—*John Bull.*

"The Author has evidently a most intimate acquaintance with the Dissenting body, and a thorough knowledge of all their quirks and oddities. . The three church clergymen—the vicar of St. Jude's, Mr. Maxworth and Mr. Deane—are all good sketches."—*Morning Post.*

"The constraints. . . . of Nonconformity are described with point and cleverness."—*World.*

"There is much matter in it that will prove interesting to many who care to look into the realities of daily life, its pains and trials. . . . . Mr. Baynard presents us with a vivid picture."—*The Queen.*

"An interesting novel, and the spirit in which it is written is very praiseworthy."—*Scotsman.*

"These volumes are very readable, and there is much in them both to amuse and instruct."—*National Church.*

"We do not believe that Mr. Baynard writes in an unkindly spirit."—*Literary World.*

"This book is readable, and the author's style is good. It has considerable interest as a testimony against Dissent in its social aspects ; and a revelation of the interior life of certain sects, whose ministers are their servants in a servile and irritating sense, unsuspected by the world outside these communities."—*Spectator.*

"The picture we have in these volumes . . . . . will come upon most readers altogether as a startling revelation of certain aspects of Voluntaryism."—*Graphic.*

RAVENSDALE. By ROBERT THYNNE, author of " Tom Delany." 3 vols., 31s. 6d.

RIDING OUT THE GALE. By ANNETTE LYSTER. 3 vols., 31s. 6d.

"The tale is full of stirring incident, and one or two of the character creations—notably Singleton's sister Hadee—are finely conceived and artistically developed."—*Scotsman.*

Samuel Tinsley & Co., 10, Southampton St., Strand.

RING OF PEARLS, THE ; or, His at Last. By
JERROLD QUICK. 2 vols., 21s.

RIVERSDALE COURT. By MRS. FORREST
GRANT, author of " Fair, but not Wise," &c. 3 vols., 31s. 6d.

RUPERT REDMOND. A Tale of England, Ire-
land, and America. By WALTER SIMS SOUTH-
WELL. 3 vols., 31s. 6d.

SAINT SIMON'S NIECE. By FRANK LEE
BENEDICT, author of " Miss Dorothy's Charge."
3 vols., 31s. 6d.
From the **Spectator**, July 24th :—"A new and powerful novelist has
arisen. . . . We rejoice to recognize a new novelist of real genius, who
knows and depicts powerfully some of the most striking and overmastering
passions of the human heart. . . . It is seldom that we rise from the perusal
of a story with the sense of excitement which Mr. Benedict has produced."

SALTHURST : a Novel. By Mrs. ARTHUR LEWIS,
author of " The Master of Riverswood." 3 vols.,
31s. 6d.

SEARCH FOR A HEART, THE : a Novel. By
JOHN ALEXANDER. 3 vols., 31s. 6d.

SECRET OF TWO HOUSES, THE. By FANNY
FISHER. 2 vols., 21s.

SEDGEBOROUGH WORLD, THE. By A. FARE-
BROTHER. 2 vols., 21s.

SELF-UNITED. By Mrs. HICKES BRYANT. 3 vols.,
31s. 6d.

SHADOW OF ERKSDALE, THE. By BOURTON
MARSHALL. 3 vols., 31s. 6d.

SHE REIGNS ALONE : a Novel. By BEATRICE
YORKE. 3 vols., 31s. 6d.

SHINGLEBOROUGH SOCIETY. 3 vols. 31s. 6d.

SIEGE OF VIENNA, THE : a Novel. By CAROLINE
PICHLER. (From the German.) 3 vols., 31s. 6d.

SIR MARMADUKE LORTON. By the Hon. A.
S. G. CANNING. 3 vols., 31s. 6d.

SOME OF OUR GIRLS. By Mrs. EILOART, author
of " The Curate's Discipline," " The Love that
Lived," " Meg," etc., etc. 3 vols., 31s. 6d.
" A book that should be read."—*Athenæum.*

SONS OF DIVES.   2 vols., 21s.

SQUIRE   HARRINGTON'S   SECRET.   By
GEORGE W. GARRETT.   2 vols., 21s.

STRANDED, BUT NOT LOST. By DOROTHY
BROMYARD.   3 vols., 31s. 6d.

ATIANA ; or, the Conspiracy. A Tale of St.
Petersburg.   By Prince JOSEPH LUBOMIRSKI.
3 vols., 31s. 6d.
"The Story is painfully interesting."—*Standard.*

THORNTONS OF THORNBURY, THE.   By
Mrs. HENRY LOWTHER CHERMSIDE.   3 vols.,
31s. 6d.

THRO' THE SHADOW.   2 vols., 21s.

TIMOTHY CRIPPLE ; or, "Life's a Feast."   By
THOMAS AURIOL ROBINSON.   2 vols., 21s.

TOO FAIR TO GO FREE. By HENRY KAY WIL-
LOUGHBY.   3 vols., 31s. 6d.

TOO LIGHTLY BROKEN.   3 vols., 31s. 6d.
"A very pleasing story. . . . very prettily told."—*Morning Post.*

TOM DELANY. By ROBERT THYNNE, author of
"Ravensdale."   3 vols., 31s. 6d.
"A very bright, healthy, simply-told story."—*Standard.*
"There is not a dull page in the book."—*Scotsman.*

TOWER HALLOWDEANE.   2 vols., 21s.

TOXIE : a Tale.   3 vols., 31s. 6d.

TRUST, THE ; an Autobiography.   By JEAN LE
PEUR.   3 vols., 31s. 6d.
To write a purely domestic tale which is so far from dull is a considerable
achievement . . . . . Each of the characters has a strongly-marked nature
of his or her own . . . . Becky Wilson is a fine portrait which must clearly
be from life.   But the book should be read."—*Athenæum.*

TRUE WOMEN. By KATHARINE STUART. 3 vols.,
31s. 6d.
"This novel is strong where so many are weak. . . . We know of no
book in which the act of courtship is made so pretty and poetical, or in
which the tenderest sentiment is so absolutely free from mawkishness."—
Standard.

'TWIXT CUP AND LIP.   By MARY LOVETT-
CAMERON.   3 vols., 31s. 6d.

'TWIXT HAMMER AND ANVIL.   By FRANK
LEE BENEDICT, author of "St. Simon's Niece,"
"Miss Dorothy's Charge," etc.   3 vols., 31s. 6d.

'TWIXT WIFE AND FATHERLAND.   2 vols.,
21s.

> " It is some one who has caught her (Baroness Tautphoeus') gift of telling
> a charming story in the boldest manner, and of forcing us to take an interest
> in her characters, which writers, far better from a literary point of view, can
> never approach."—*Athenæum.*

TWO STRIDES OF DESTINY.   By S. BROOKES
BUCKLEE.   3 vols., 31s. 6d.

UNDER PRESSURE.   By T. E. PEMBERTON,
2 vols., 21s.   ,

VERY OLD QUESTION, A: a Novel.   By
T. EDGAR PEMBERTON, Author of "Under
Pressure," &c.   3 vols., 31s. 6d.

> " For 'tis a question left us yet to prove,
> Whether love lead fortune or else fortune love."—*Hamlet.*

WAGES: a Story.   3 vols., 31s. 6d.

WANDERING FIRES.   By Mrs. M. C. DESPARD,
author of "Chaste as Ice," &c.   3 vols., 31s. 6d.

WEIMAR'S TRUST.   By Mrs. EDWARD CHRISTIAN.
3 vols., 31s. 6d.

WHAT OLD FATHER THAMES SAID.   By
COUTTS NELSON.   3 vols., 31s. 6d.

WIDOW UNMASKED, THE; or, the Firebrand
in the Family.   By FLORA F. WYLDE.   3 vols.,
31s. 6d.

WILL SHE BEAR IT?   A Tale of the Weald.
3 vols., 31s. 6d.

> This is a clever story, easily and naturally told, and the reader's
> interest sustained throughout. . . . A pleasant, readable book, such as
> we can heartily recommend."—*Spectator.*

Samuel Tinsley & Co., 10, Southampton St., Strand.

WOMAN TO BE WON, A. An Anglo-Indian Sketch. By ATHENE BRAMA. 2 vols, 21s.

"She is a woman, therefore may be wooed ;
She is a woman, therefore may be won."
—TITUS ANDRONICUS, Act ii., Sc. 1.

"A welcome addition to the literature connected with the most picturesque of our dependencies."—*Athenæum.*

"As a tale of adventure "A Woman to be Won " is entitled to decided commendation."—*Graphic.*

"A more familiar sketch of station life in India . . . . has never been written. . . ."—*Nonconformist.*

POPULAR NEW NOVELS, &c.,
EACH COMPLETE IN ONE VOLUME.

DAM AND EVE'S COURTSHIP; or how to Write a Novel. By JAY WYE. Crown 8vo., 7s. 6d.

ADVENTURES OF MICK CALLIGHIN, M.P., THE. A Story of Home Rule; THE DE BURGHOS, a Romance. By W. R. ANCKETILL. In one Volume, with Illustrations. Crown 8vo., 7s. 6d.

AS THE FATES WOULD HAVE IT. By G. BERESFORD FITZGERALD. Crown 8vo., 10s. 6d.

ORN TO BE A LADY. By KATHERINE HENDERSON. Crown 8vo., price 7s. 6d.

BREAD UPON THE WATERS: a Novel. By MARIE J. HYDE. Crown 8vo., 7s. 6d.

BRIDE OF ROERVIG, THE. By W. BERGSOE. Translated from the Danish by NINA FRANCIS. Crown 8vo., 7s. 6d.

"A charmingly fresh and simple tale, which was well worth translating, and has been translated well."—*Athenæum.*

"There is a strong human interest throughout the story, and it abounds with little snatches of description, which are full of poetic grace and charm. . . . The translator has been most successful in preserving the spirit and genuine Norse flavour of the original."—*Scotsman.*

BRITISH SUBALTERN, THE. By an EX-SUBALTERN. One vol., 7s. 6d.

BURIED PAST, THE : a Novel. Crown 8vo, price 7s. 6d.

"In the short space at our command it is impossible to do this volume justice. It is a pleasant change from the highly-coloured sensationalism of the present day, and we can faithfully pronounce it the best novel we have read for some time."—*Civil Service Gazette.*

Samuel Tinsley & Co., 10, Southampton St., Strand.

BUILDING UPON SAND.   By ELIZABETH J.
LYSAGHT.   Crown 8vo., 10s. 6d.

BROAD OUTLINES OF LONG YEARS IN
AUSTRALIA.   By Mrs. HENRY JONES, of Binnum Binnum.
Crown 8vo., 7s. 6d.
" Gives a very pleasant picture of life in the Australian bush. . . . We
recommend the volume to intending emigrants, not only as containing
plenty of practical advice, but as likely to give them cheerful anticipations
of the life before them, when its first inevitable roughness is over."—
John Bull.

CHRISTIERN THE WICKED : an Historical
Tale.   By H. S. TAGSON.   (The Author's Translation.)
Crown 8vo., 7s. 6d.

CINDERELLA : a new version of an old Story.
Crown 8vo., 7s. 6d.

CLARA PONSONBY : a Novel.   By ROBERT BEV-
ERIDGE.   1 vol. crown 8vo., 7s. 6d.

CLEWBEND, THE.   By MOY ELLA.' Crown 8vo.,
7s. 6d.

COOMB DESERT.   By G. W. FITZ.   Crown 8vo.,
7s. 6d.

CORALIA ; a Plaint of Futurity.   By the Author of
" Pyrna."   Crown 8vo., 7s. 6d.

DAISY AND THE EARL.   By CONSTANCE
HOWELL.   Crown 8vo. 7s. 6d.
" A cleverly and thoughtfully-written book, in which a subject comparatively new is handled with much knowledge of human nature, and with
real grace of manner, is ' Daisy and the Earl.' . . . . A very enjoyable
volume."—*Scotsman.*

DISCORD, A : a Story.   By ALETH WILLESON.
1 vol., crown 8vo., 7s. 6d.
" Something more than ordinary praise is due to a story which has a
leading idea of its own, and works it out steadily, yet without wearying the
reader with excessive iteration or exaggeration. . . . . ' A Discord ' reminds
us of some of Miss Sewell's best works. We should almost be disposed to
give it the preference, on the ground that the human interest is broader.
Sometimes we see traces of another and well-known influence. Mr. Price
is a person not unworthy of the gallery of portraits which George Eliot has
given to us."—*Spectator.*

DISINTERRED.   From the Boke of a Monk of
Carden Abbey.   By T. ESMONDE.   Crown 8vo, 7s. 6d.

EARL OF EFFINGHAM, THE.   By LALLA
M'DOWELL, Author of " How we learned to Help
Ourselves."   Crown 8vo., 7s. 6d.

Samuel Tinsley & Co., 10, Southampton St., Strand.

EMERGING FROM THE CHRYSALIS. By J. F. NICHOLLS. Crown 8vo., 7s. 6d.

AIR MAID OF TAUNTON, THE : a Tale of the Siege. By ELIZABETH M. ALFORD. Crown 8vo., 6s.

FERNVALE : Some Pages of Elsie's Life. By HARRY BUCHANAN. Crown 8vo, 7s. 6d.

FLORENCE ; or Loyal Quand Même. By FRANCES ARMSTRONG. Crown 8vo, 5s., cloth. Post free.

"A very charming love story, eminently pure and lady-like in tone."— *Civil Service Review.*

FOR TWO YEARS. By VECTIS. Crown 8vo, 7s. 6d.

FRIEDEMANN BACH ; or, the Fortunes of an Idealist. Adapted from the German of A. E. BRACHVOGEL. By the Rev. J. WALKER, B.C.L. Dedicated, with permission, to H.R.H. the PRINCESS CHRISTIAN of SCHLESWIG-HOL-STEIN. I vol., crown 8vo, 7s. 6d.

FROM A BED OF ROSES. By CUTHBERT HOPE. Crown 8vo, 7s. 6d.

REGORS, THE : a Cornish Story. By JANE H. SPETTIGUE. Crown 8vo., 7s. 6d.

ARRINGTON ; or, the Exiled Royalist : a tale of the Hague. By FREDERICK SPENCER BIRD. Crown 8vo., price 7s. 6d.

NSIDIOUS THIEF, THE : a Tale for Humble Folks. By One of Themselves. Crown 8vo, 5s. Second Edition.

IN TROPIC SEAS : a Tale of the Spanish Main. By W. WESTALL. Author of " Tales and Legends of Saxony and Lusatia." Crown 8vo., 7s. 6d.

IN THE SPRING OF MY LIFE : a Love Story. By the Princess OLGA CANTACUZÈNE. Translated from the French by Madame KLAUS, with the author's approval. Crown 8vo., 7s. 6d.

INTRICATE PATHS. By C. L. J. S. Crown 8vo, 7s. 6d.

OHN FENN'S WIFE. By MARIA LEWIS. Crown 8vo, 7s. 6d.

ADY BLANCHE, THE. By HAROLD ST. CLAIR. Crown 8vo, 7s. 6d.

LALAGE. By AUGUSTA CHAMBERS. Crown 8vo, 7s. 6d.

LEAVES FROM AN OLD PORTFOLIO. By ELIZA MARY BARRON. Crown 8vo, 7s. 6d.

LITTLE ALPINE FOX-DOG, THE: a Love Story. By CECIL CLARKE. Crown 8vo, 7s. 6d.

LILIAN. By G. BERESFORD FITZ GERALD, author of "As the Fates Would Have It." Crown 8vo, 7s. 6d.

LIFE AND ADVENTURES OF AN UNFORTU-NATE AUTHOR, THE. Written by Himself. Crown 8vo. 7s. 6d.

LOVED AND UNLOVED : a Story. By HARRIET DAVIS. Crown 8vo., 7s. 6d.

LOVE THE LEVELLER : a Tale. Crown 8vo, 7s. 6d.

MARGARET MORTIMER'S SECOND HUS-BAND. By Mrs. HILLS. 1 vol., 7s. 6d.

MARJORY'S FAITH. By FLORENCE HARDING. Crown 8vo, 7s. 6d.

MARRIED FOR MONEY. 1 vol., 10s. 6d.

MARTIN LAWS : a Story. Crown 8vo., 7s. 6d.

MAUD LEATHWAITE : an Autobiography. By BEATRICE A. JOURDAN, author of "The Journal of a Waiting Gentlewoman." Crown 8vo., 7s. 6d.

MERRY AND GRAVE. By PETER ATHELBY. Crown 8vo, 7s. 6d.

MILES : a Town Story. By SIGMA. Author of "Fan." Crown 8vo., 5s.

MISTRESS OF LANGDALE HALL, THE : a Romance of the West Riding. By ROSA MACKENZIE KETTLE. Complete in one handsome volume, with Frontispiece and Vignette by PERCIVAL SKELTON. 4s., post free.

"The story is interesting and very pleasantly written, and for the sake of both author and publisher, we cordially wish it the reception it deserves." —*Saturday Review.*

Samuel Tinsley & Co., 10, Southampton St., Strand.

MUSICAL TALES, PHANTASMS, AND
SKETCHES. From the German of ELISE POLKO. BY M.
PRIME MAUDSLAY. Dedicated (with permission) to Sir
Julius Benedict. Crown 8vo., 7s. 6d.
Also Second Series of the above, uniform in size and price.

NEGLECTED; a Story of Nursery Education
Forty Years Ago. By Miss JULIA LUARD. Crown
8vo., 5s., cloth.

NEW-FASHIONED TORY, A. By "WEST
SOMERSET." 1 vol., crown 8vo., 7s. 6d.

NORTONDALE CASTLE. 1 vol., 7s. 6d.

NOT TO BE BROKEN. By W. A. CHANDLER.
Crown 8vo., 10s. 6d.

ONE FOR ANOTHER. By EMMA C. WAIT.
Crown 8vo., 7s. 6d.

PUTTYPUT'S PROTEGEE; or Road, Rail, and
River. A Story in Three Books. By HENRY GEORGE
CHURCHILL. Crown 8vo., (uniform with "The Mistress of Langdale Hall"), with 14 illustrations by WALLIS
MACKAY. Post free, 4s. Second edition.
" "It is a lengthened and diversified farce, full of screaming fun and comic
delineation—a reflection of Dickens, Mrs. Malaprop, and Mr. Boucicault,
and dealing with various descriptions of social life. We have read and
laughed, pooh-poohed, and read again, ashamed of our interest, but our
interest has been too strong for our shame. Readers may do worse than
surrender themselves to its melo-dramatic enjoyment. From title-page to
colophon, only Dominie Sampson's epithet can describe it—it is 'pro-
digious.'"—*British Quarterly Review.*

REAL AND UNREAL: Tales of Both Kinds.
By HARRIET OLIVIA BODDINGTON. Crown 8vo., 7s. 6d.

REIGN OF ROSAS, THE, or South American
Sketches. By E. C. FERNAU. Crown 8vo., 7s. 6d.

REGENT ROSALIND: a Story. By the author of
" Workaday Briars," &c. Crown 8vo., 7s. 6d.

RENRUTH. By HENRY TURNER. Crown 8vo.,
7s. 6d.

ROSIE AND HUGH; or, Lost and Found. By
HELEN C. NASH. 1 vol., crown 8vo., 6s.

SACRIFICE TO HONOUR, A. By Mrs. HENRY
LYTTELTON ROGERS. Crown 8vo., 7s. 6d.

ST. NICHOLAS' EVE, and other Tales.   By MARY
C. ROWSELL.   Crown 8vo., 7s. 6d.

SIBYLLE'S   STORY.   By OCTAVE   FEUILLET.
Translated by MARGARET WATSON.   Crown 8vo., 7s. 6d.

SIR   AUBYN'S   HOUSEHOLD.   By   SIGMA.
Author of " Fan."   Crown 8vo., 7s. 6d.

SKYWARD AND EARTHWARD: a Tale.   By
ARTHUR PENRICE.   1 vol.   Crown 8vo., 7s. 6d.

SOPHIA : a Novel.   By JANE ASHTON.   Crown
8vo., 7s. 6d.

SO SINKS THE DAY STAR : The Story of Two
Lovings and a Liking.   By JAMES KEITH.   Crown 8vo.,
7s. 6d.

SPOILT LIVES.   By Mrs. RAPER.   Cr. 8vo., 7s. 6d.

STANLEY MEREDITH : a Tale by " SABINA."
Crown 8vo., 7s. 6d.

STAR OF HOPE, THE, and other Tales.   By VIC-
TORIA STEWART.   Crown 8vo., 7s. 6d.

STILL UNSURE.   By C. VANE, Author of " Sweet
Bells Jangled."   Crown 8vo., 7s. 6d.

SWEET IDOLATRY.   By Miss ANSTRUTHER.
Crown 8vo., 7s. 6d.

SURGEON'S SECRET, THE.   By SYDNEY MOS-
TYN, Author of " Kitty's Rival," etc.   Crown 8vo., 10s. 6d.

" A most exciting novel—the best on our list.   It may be fairly recommended as a very extraordinary book."—*John Bull.*

SUSSEX IDYL, A.   By CLEMENTINA BLACK.
Crown 8vo., 7s. 6d.

THROUGH HARDSHIPS TO LORDSHIPS.
By FLORA EATON.   Crown 8vo., 7s. 6d.

TEN TIMES PAID : a Story of the South.   By
BRUTON BLOSSE.   Crown 8vo., 7s. 6d.

TIM'S CHARGE.   By AMY CAMPBELL.   1 vol.,
Crown 8vo., 7s. 6d.

TOUCH NOT THE NETTLE : a Story.   By ALEC
FEARON.   Crown 8vo., 7s. 6d.

TRUE STORY OF HUGH NOBLE'S FLIGHT,
THE.   By the Authoress of " What Her Face Said."   10s. 6d.

NTO WHICH SHE WAS NOT BORN· By ELLEN GADESDEN. Crown 8vo., 7s. 6d.

"A trouble weighed upon her and perplexed her night and morn,
With the burden of an honour unto which she was not born."
TENNYSON.

AGABOND CHARLIE. By "VAGABOND."
1 vol. crown 8vo., 7s. 6d.

VANDELEURS OF RED TOR, The. A Tale of
South Devon. By THEODORE RUSSELL MONRO. Crown 8vo.,
7s. 6d.

VANESSA FAIRE. By GEORGE JOSEPH. Crown
8vo., 7s. 6d.

EBS OF LOVE. (I. A Lawyer's Device. II.
Sancta Simplicitas.) By G. E. H. 1 vol., Crown 8vo.,
10s. 6d.

WHO CAN TELL? By MERE HAZARD. Crown
8vo., 7s. 6d.

WIDOW OF WINDSOR, A. By ANNIE GASKELL.
Crown 8vo., 7s. 6d.

WOMAN THAT SHALL BE PRAISED, THE:
a Novel. By HILDA REAY. 1 vol., Crown 8vo., 7s. 6d.

"Decidedly well written, attractive, and readable. . . . The characters
stand out as if they had been pondered over and worked at; the circumstances are fresh and natural; the style is pure, and the thoughts refined."
—*Athenæum.*

"Besides the heroine there is another 'woman that shall be praised,'
viz., the authoress. Praised for writing in English, for some passages of
poetry, for some even of slang, for her boldness and tenderness of expression,
and, above all, for writing a religious novel without shocking us with pious
utterances."—*Public Opinion.*

WOMAN'S AMBITION. By M. L. LYONS. 1 vol.,
7s. 6d.

E OUTSIDE FOOLS; or, Glimpses Inside
the Stock Exchange. By ERASMUS PINTO, Broker.
Crown 8vo., 5s.

"Written in a clever, cynical, and incisive style, and thoroughly exposes
the 'rigs' and tricks of the Stock Exchange. One advantage of a perusal
will be that those who allow themselves to be plundered will do so quite
consciously. The volume as a whole is extremely interesting."—*Public
Opinion.*

YE VAMPYRES! A Legend of the National
Betting Ring, showing what became of it. By the SPECTRE.
In striking Illustrated Cover, price 2s., post free.

YOUTH OF THE PERIOD, THE. By J. F. SHAW
KENNEDY, Esq., late 79th Highlanders. Crown 8vo., 7s. 6d.

BOOKS OF TRAVEL &c.

TWO YEARS OF THE EASTERN QUES-
TION. By A. GALLENGA (of the *Times*), author of
"Italy Revisited," "Country Life in Piedmont," "The
Invasion of Denmark," etc. 2 vols., 8vo., price 30s.

The **Times** says :—"A more thorough exposure of the rottenness of the
Turkish System was never penned ; and Mr. Freeman and Mr. Gladstone
must rejoice when they peruse page after page which, to use a familiar expression, does not leave on the Turks ' the face of a dog.' . . . . . But Mr.
Gallenga did not visit Constantinople to quarrel, but to observe the various
phases of the Eastern Question as it passed from diplomatic remonstrances
to provincial outbreaks, to Bulgarian atrocities, to the Servian war, to the
Armistice, to the Conference, to renewed Protocols, and at last to this war
between Russia and Turkey. . . . . . Extraordinary opportunities fell into
Mr. Gallenga's way, and in these very interesting volumes he has availed
himself of them to the full."

The **Observer** says :—"The great merit of these two interesting volumes
is that they present the grave considered judgment of an intelligent, thoughtful observer on the internal condition of Turkey. . . For anyone who would
really know the social forces now at work within the Turkish Empire, and
who would aspire to make any intelligent forecast as to its future fate,
these volumes are invaluable guides. . . . The book is at once fascinating
and amusing, and in many ways the best recent contribution to the literature
of the Eastern Question."

The **Saturday Review** says :—"Mr. Gallenga's reminiscences of the East
are both agreeable and instructive. Notwithstanding his long practice as
an English writer, it is surprising that a foreigner should have acquired the
command of style and literary skill which are displayed in his present work
as in many former publications."

The **Graphic** says :—"Mr. Gallenga's letters are most interesting in
every way—bright with the genuine freshness of a correspondent who finds
himself on (to him) new ground, and enjoys as much as any of his readers a
moonlight ride round Stamboul, a visit to the fields of Troy, a sight of the
Sultan opening his Parliament; valuable for descriptions, by a trained
observer, of scenes and Institutions which fell beneath his eye, and specu-
lations, by a well informed politician, on the scruples and suspicions which
have ended in keeping Europe impotent while Russia and Turkey are
closing hand to hand. . . . . . Two volumes, altogether, which bid fair to
acquire permanent value as graphic records taken on the spot of some of
the most dramatic incidents in history."

The **Academy** says :—"Mr. Gallenga has given a detailed account of the
circumstances which led to the present war, beginning from the commence-
of the insurrection in the Herzegovina. As he resided in Constantinople
during the whole of this period, and had special facilities for obtaining information as the correspondent of the *Times* newspaper, his narrative is of
great value. He went there with an unprejudiced mind, having, in fact,
given but little attention to the subject until that time. . . . Mr. Gallenga also
initiates us into most of the questions relating to Turkey, on which the
reader desires an unbiassed opinion—the good and bad of the character of
the Turks themselves, their finances, their reforms, their relation to the
subject races, and the principal influences that are at work among them. . .
But the interest of his narrative culminates in that group of events which are
exciting enough for any work of fiction."

ITALY REVISITED. By A. GALLENGA. Author

of "Italy, Past and Present," "Country Life in Piedmont,"
etc.   2 vols., demy 8vo., 30s. Second Edition.

Times, Nov. 11, 1875.—"Mr. Gallenga's new volumes on Italy will be
welcome to those who care for an unprejudiced account of the prospects and
present condition of the country. . . .In noticing Mr. Gallenga's most
interesting volumes, we have been obliged to confine ourselves chiefly to
topics of grave and national importance, and we wish we could also have
done justice to his impressions of the Italy he revisited as seen in its lighter
and social aspects."

Spectator, Nov. 20, 1875.—"The two volumes abound in interesting
matter, with vivid sketches of places and persons,—Florence for instance,—
Garibaldi and Mazzini. The personal reminiscences, too, of the author's
bloodless campaign with Prince Napoleon in 1859 are notably interesting."

Observer, Nov. 7, 1875.—"*Facile princeps* in the ranks of those who
have laboured, through the influential channel of journalism, to arouse the
sympathies of the world for the kingdom of Italy, and to enable it to judge
of Italy's condition and Italy's prospects, has been, and still is, Mr. Gallenga.
It would be wonderful if any one could pretend to be his rival."

Athenæum, Nov. 20, 1875.—"Mr. Gallenga's two volumes are as distinctly superior to the usual newspaper correspondent's platitudes, as they
are free from the egotistical garrulities with which tourists, and especially
tourists in Italy, have made us familiar."

Daily News, Dec. 3, 1875.—"Is beyond comparison the most readable,
and at the same time, the most trustworthy account of the actual condition
and prospects of a nation and kingdom which but yesterday were a dream
of visionaries, and to-day are among the most potent and practical realities
of the modern world. . . . The lightest or the most serious reader may find
plenty of attractive matter in these varied and suggestive pages, from the
liveliest stories to the weightiest economic considerations and statistics."

World, Dec. 1, 1875.—"Were there to be a judgment of Paris among
the rivalries of modern journalists, the three competitors would, we suppose,
have to be Mr. Gallenga, Mr. Sala, and Mr. Russell, and we should award
the apple without hesitation to Mr. Gallenga. He is the best informed, the
most accurate, the most highly educated, the best linguist, the most variously
experienced of the three. . . . His is by far the most classic pen, and the
best measured style. He has just published a couple of entertaining and
instructive volumes."

UNTRODDEN SPAIN, and her Black Country.

Being Sketches of the Life and Character of the Spaniard of
the Interior. By HUGH JAMES ROSE, M.A., of Oriel College,
Oxford. In 2 vols., 8vo., price 30s. (*Second Edition.*)

The **Times** says—"These volumes form a very pleasing commentary on
a land and a people to which Englishmen will always turn with sympathetic
interest."

The **Saturday Review** says—"His title of 'Untrodden Spain' is no
misnomer. He leads us into scenes and among classes of Spaniards where few
English writers have preceded him. . . . We can only recommend our
readers to get it and search for themselves. Those who are most intimately
acquainted with Spain will best appreciate its varied excellence."

The **Spectator** says—"The author's kindliness is as conspicuous as his
closeness of observation and fairness of judgment ; his sympathy with the
people inspires his pen as happily as does his artistic appreciation of the
country ; and both have combined in the production of a work of striking
novelty and sterling value."

6   **Samuel Tinsley and Co.'s Publications.**

The **Standard** says—"It is fresh, life-like, and chatty, and is written by a man who is accustomed to look below the surface of things."

The **Athenæum** says—"We regret that we cannot make further extracts, for 'Untrodden Spain' is by far the best book upon Spanish peasant life that we have ever met with."

The **Literary Churchman** says—"Seldom has a book of travel come before us which has so taken our fancy in reading, and left behind it, when the reading was over, so distinct an impression. . . . We must reluctantly close our review of these delightful volumes, leaving the major part of them unnoticed. But we have quoted sufficient to show our readers how well the author has used his opportunities."

The **Nonconformist** says—"This book forms most interesting reading. It is the result of careful observation, it communicates many facts, it is written in a polished yet lively style, and will thus, perhaps, remain for some time the best reference-book about rural Spain."

The **Field** says—"An amount of really valuable information respecting the lower classes of Spaniards, their daily life and conversation, and ways of looking at things, such as few writers have given us."

The **John Bull** says—"We have rarely been able to recommend a book more cordially. It has not a dull page. . . . Deserves to be a great success."

OVER THE BORDERS OF CHRISTENDOM AND

ESLAMIAH; or, Travels in the Summer of 1875 through Hungary, Slavonia, Servia, Bosnia, Herzegovina, Dalmatia, and Montenegro to the North of Albania. By JAMES CREAGH, author of 'A Scamper to Sebastopol.' 2 vols., large post 8vo. 25s.

Public Opinion, Dec. 11, 1875.—"Nothing appears to have escaped Captain Creagh's observant eyes and ears, and his narrative has all the charm of a well-written romance."

Daily News.—"He went down the Danube to Belgrade, thence, turning westward, took his passage in a steam vessel up the river Save, and at Brod penetrated southward into Bosnia, visiting Bosna-Serai and Mostar, and thus coming in sight of the Adriatic at Ragusa."

Graphic.—"A rollicking tale of an Irishman's scamper from Pesth to Belgrade, thence up the Save to Brod, a town half Austrian half Turk, and down through the heart of the now insurgents' districts to Ragusa and Montenegro."

Figaro.—"The attention that has been so recently directed to Herzegovina gives a peculiar interest to Capt. Creagh's lively narrative and adventurous journey, and his two volumes will be received as a welcome addition to modern books of travel."

World.—"A new and seasonable book of travels. Captain Creagh has recently been tramping through Hungary, Slavonia, Servia, Bosnia, Herzegovina, Dalmatia, Montenegro, and a few other comparatively unknown countries."

Athenæum.—"The record of travel consists partly of descriptions of out-of-the-way places, where few except the writer have been, and which he can depict at his will. . . . His volumes will be welcome."

Scotsman.—"Mr. Creagh is an old traveller, with a considerable faculty of observation; his style is racy, and he has much humour. . . Clever and decidedly readable."

Samuel Tinsley & Co., 10, Southampton St., Strand.

CANTON AND THE BOGUE: the Narrative of
an eventful six months in China. By WALTER WILLIAM MUNDY. Crown 8vo., 7s. 6d.

TRAVEL AND SPORT IN BURMAH, SIAM,
AND THE MALAY PENINSULA. By JOHN BRADLEY. Post 8vo., 12s.

TO THE DESERT AND BACK; or Travels in
Spain, the Barbary States, Italy, etc., in 1875-76. By ZOUCH H. TURTON. One vol. large post 8vo. 12s.

New and Cheaper Edition of Mr. Minturn's "Travels West."

TRAVELS WEST. By WILLIAM MINTURN. Large
post 8vo., price 7s. 6d.

The **Daily News** says—"An unpretending volume of travel, the author of which describes in a lively vein what he saw and heard in a recent journey from New York to St. Louis, thence to Salt Lake City and California, and back by Omaha and Chicago into Canada."

Public Opinion says—"A charming book, full of anecdotes of Western American travel, and in which, the author, who travelled from New York across the whole American Western desert, gives his experience of a country almost unknown to European colonists. We wish we could transcribe some of the very clear descriptions of scenery, life, and manners in which this book abounds."

The **Queen** says—"Mr. Minturn writes easily and pleasantly, and gives us vivid pictures of the marvellous scenery. . . . . The whole tone of Mr. Minturn's book is pleasant to the English reader. . . in a word, good sense and culture contribute to make the volume well worth the attention of those who are interested in travel on the American Continent."

Vanity Fair says—"Some of our ablest authors have failed in the endeavour to depict American life and society. The author of the present work, however, is an American by birth who has spent most of his life in Europe, and he describes his return to America and his tour through the States in a very interesting volume. . . . . . Altogether the work is well-written and interesting."

The **Literary World** says—"A trip across America is a grand thing for the tourist, English or American, in the course of his career. Anyone contemplating such a journey should have a look at Mr. Minturn's book."

AMONG THE CARLISTS. By JOHN FURLEY,
author of "Struggles and Experiences of a Neutral Volunteer." Crown 8vo. 7s. 6d.

HOW I SPENT MY TWO YEARS' LEAVE; or,
My Impressions of the Mother Country, the Continent of Europe, the United States of America, and Canada. By an Indian Officer. In one vol., 8vo. Price 12s.

SYRIA AND EGYPT UNDER THE LAST FIVE
SULTANS OF TURKEY; being the Experiences during fifty years of Mr. Consul-General Barker, with explanatory remarks to the present day, by his son, EDWARD B. B. BARKER, H.B.M. Consul. In 2 vols. 8vo.

ROBA D'ITALIA ; or, Italian Lights and Shadows : a record of Travel. By CHARLES W. HECKETHORN. In 2 vols., 8vo., price 30s.

MALTA SIXTY YEARS AGO. With a Concise History of the Order of St. John of Jerusalem, the Crusades, and Knights Templars. By Col. CLAUDIUS SHAW. Handsomely bound in cloth, 10s. 6d., gilt edges, 12s.

MISCELLANEOUS..

SLAM ; its Origin, Genius, and Mission. By JOHN JOSEPH LAKE, author of "Notes and Essays on the Christian Religion." Crown 8vo., price 5s.

ANOTHER WORLD ; or, Fragments from the Star City of Montalluyah. By HERMES. Third Edition, revised, with additions. Post 8vo., price 12s.

DICKENS'S LONDON : or, London in the Works of Charles Dickens. By T. EDGAR PEMBERTON, author of "Under Pressure." Crown 8vo., 6s.

EPITAPHIANA ; or, the Curiosities of Churchyard Literature : being a Miscellaneous Collection of Epitaphs, with an INTRODUCTION. By W. FAIRLEY. Crown 8vo., cloth, price 5s. Post free.
" Entertaining."—*Pall Mall Gazette.*
" A capital collection."—*Court Circular.*
" A very readable volume."—*Daily Review.*
" A most interesting book."—*Leeds Mercury.*
" Interesting and amusing."—*Nonconformist.*
" Particularly entertaining."—*Public Opinion.*
" A curious and entertaining volume."—*Oxford Chronicle.*
" A very interesting collection."—*Civil Service Gazette.*

ETYMONIA. In 1 vol., crown 8vo., 7s. 6d.

FACT AGAINST FICTION. The Habits and Treatment of Animals Practically Considered. Hydrophobia and Distemper. With some remarks on Darwin. By the HON. GRANTLEY F. BERKELEY. 2 vols. 8vo., 30s.

MOVING EARS. By the Ven. Archdeacon WEAKHEAD, Rector of Newtown, Kent. 1 vol., crown 8vo., 5s.

NOTES AND ESSAYS ON THE CHRISTIAN RELIGION : Its Philosophical Principles and its Enemies. By JOHN JOSEPH LAKE. Crown 8vo., price 7s. 6d.

OUR INDIAN EMPIRE : the History of the Wonderful Rise of British Supremacy in Hindustan. By the Rev. SAMUEL NORWOOD, B.A., Head Master of the Grammar School, Whalley. Crown 8vo., 7s. 6d.

SOCIAL ARCHITECTURE; or, Reasons and Means for the Demolition and Reconstruction of the Social Edifice. By AN EXILE FROM FRANCE. Demy 8vo., 16s.

THERESE HENNES, AND HER MUSICAL EDUCATION : a Biographical Sketch. By her FATHER. Translated from the German MS. by H. MANNHEIMER. Crown 8vo., 5s.

THE PHYSIOLOGY OF THE SECTS. Crown 8vo., price 5s.

THE RISE AND DECAY OF THE RULE OF ISLAM. By ARCHIBALD J. DUNN. Large post 8vo., 12s.

POETRY, &c.

ARVELON : a Poem. By W. J. DAWSON. Fcp. 8vo., 4s. 6d.

DEATH OF ÆGEUS, THE, and other Poems. By W. H. A. EMRA. Fcp. 8vo., 5s.

EMPEROR AND THE GALILEAN, THE : a Drama in two parts. Translated from the Norwegian of HENRIK IBSEN, by CATHERINE RAY. In 1 vol., crown 8vo., 7s. 6d.

FARM, THE : Incidents and Occurrences thereat. By D. W. SLANN. With Songs and Music. Crown 8vo., price 6s.

FAREWELL TO LIFE ; or Lyrical Reminiscences of British Peers in Art. With a Biographical Sketch of the late Patrick Nasmyth. By RICHARD LANGLEY. Dedicated to Sir Francis Grant, President of the Royal Academy. Fcp. 8vo., price 3s. 6d.

GRANADA, AND OTHER POEMS. By M. SABISTON. Fcp. 8vo., 4s.

HELEN, and other Poems. By HUBERT CURTIS. Fcp. 8vo., 3s. 6d.

MARY DESMOND, AND OTHER POEMS. By NICHOLAS J. GANNON. Fcp. 8vo., 4s., cloth. Second Edition.

MISPLACED LOVE. A Tale of Love, Sin, Sorrow, and Remorse. 1 vol., crown 8vo., 5s.

POEMS AND SONNETS. By H. Greenhough Smith, B.A. Fcp. 8vo., 3s. 6d.

REGENT, The: a Play in Five Acts and Epilogue. By J. M. Chanson. Crown 8vo., 5s.

RITUALIST'S PROGRESS, The; or, a Sketch of the Reforms and Ministrations of the Rev. Septimus Alban, Member of the E.C.U., Vicar of S. Alicia, Sloperton. By A B Wildered Parishioner. Fcp. 8vo., 2s. 6d., cloth.

SOUL SPEAKS, The, and other Poems. By Francis H. Hemery. In wrapper, 1s.

SUMMER SHADE AND WINTER SUNSHINE: Poems. By Rosa Mackenzie Kettle, author of "The Mistress of Langdale Hall." New Edition. 2s. 6d., cloth.

WITCH OF NEMI, The, and other Poems. By Edward Brennan. Crown 8vo., 10s. 6d.

PAMPHLETS, &c.

ALFRED THE GREAT: an Opera in Four Acts. By Isaac Hearnden. In wrapper, price 1s.

ALPERTON GHOST, The: a Story. By Miss F. H. Waldy. Price 6d., post free.

ANOTHER ROW AT DAME EUROPA'S SCHOOL. Showing how John's Cook made an Irish Stew, and what came of it. 6d., sewed.

"ANY WOMAN WILL DO FOR A MAN:" a Warning to those about to Marry. In wrapper, 6d., post free. (Now ready, New Edition, price 3d.)

BALAK AND BALAAM IN EUROPEAN COSTUME. By the Rev. James Kean, M.A., Assistant to the Incumbent of Markinch, Fife. 6d., sewed.

BATTLE OF THE TITLE, The: showing how Will Happirok and Tommy Hyghe tried to get into office and failed. In wrapper, 1s., post free.

CONFESSIONS OF A WEST-END USURER. In illustrated cover, price 1s., post free.

DIFFICULTIES OF POLITICAL ECONOMY. By a Young Beginner. Crown 8vo., 2s. 6d.

ETERNAL PUNISHMENT. The Doctrine of the Everlasting Torment of the Wicked shown to be Unscriptural. In wrapper, 1s., post free.

FALL OF MAN, THE : an Answer to Mr. Darwin's "Descent of Man ;" being a Complete Refutation, by common-sense arguments, of the Theory of Natural Selection. 1s., sewed.

GOLDEN PATH, THE : a Poem. By ISABELLA STUART. 6d., sewed.

GREAT FIGHT, THE, BETWEEN THE BEAR AND THE TURKEY. Its Origin and Probable Results. By a YOUNG LION. In wrapper, price 6d., post free.

HOW THE FIRE WAS KINDLED, AND HOW THE WATER BOILED ; or, Lessons in Agitation. In wrapper, 1s.

IRISH COLLAPSE, THE ; or, Three Months of Home Rule : Vision of Confusion. Dedicated to the Right Hon. the Earl of Beaconsfield. By the MEMBER FOR DONNY-BROOK. In wrapper, 1s., post free.

LETTER TO THE QUEEN, A, ON HER RETIREMENT FROM PUBLIC LIFE. By One of Her Majesty's most Loyal Subjects. In wrapper, price 1s., post free.

MISTRESSES AND MAIDS. By HUBERT CURTIS, author of "Helen," &c. Price 1d.

NEW ZEALANDER, THE, ON LONDON BRIDGE ; or, Moral Ruins of the Modern Babylon. By a M.L.C. In wrapper, price 1s.

OLD TABLE, THE : a Story for the Young. In wrapper, 1s., post free.

ON THE MISMANAGEMENT OF THE PUBLIC RECORD OFFICE. By J. PYM YEATMAN, Barrister-at-Law. In wrapper, price 1s.

OLD CHURCH KEY, THE. By the Rev. W. H. A. EMRA. In wrapper, price 6d., post free.

PUZZLES FOR LEISURE HOURS, Original and Selected. Edited by THOMAS OWEN. In ornamental wrapper, price 1s., post free.

REAL AND THE IDEAL, THE, THE BEAUTI-FUL AND THE TRUE ; or, Art in the Nineteenth Century : a Plain Treatise for Plain People, containing a new and startling Revelation for the Pre-Raphaelites. By a RUSTIC RUSKIN. 2s. 6d.

REDBREAST OF CANTERBURY CATHE-DRAL, THE : Lines from the Latin of Peter du Moulin, sometime a Prebendary of Canterbury. Translated by the Rev. F. B. Wells, M.A., Rector of Woodchurch. Handsomely bound, price 1s.

SKETCHES IN CORNWALL.   By M. F. Bragge.
In Wrapper, price 1s.

TICHBORNE AND ORTON AUTOGRAPHS,
THE ; comprising Autograph Letters of Roger Tichborne,
Arthur Orton (to Mary Ann Loder), and the Defendant (early,
letters to Lady Tichborne, &c.), in facsimile.   In wrapper,
price 6d.

TWELVE NATIONAL BALLADS (First Series).
Dedicated to Liberals of all classes.   By Philhelot, of
Cambridge.   In ornamental cover, price 6d., post free.

TRUE FLEMISH STORY, A.   By the author o˙˙
"The Eve of St. Nicholas."   In wrapper, 1s.

USE AND ABUSE OF IRRATIONAL ANI-
MALS, THE ; with some Remarks on the Essential Moral
Difference between Genuine "Sport" and the Horrors of
Vivisection.   In wrapper, price 1s., post free.

BOOKS FOR THE YOUNG.

ADVENTURES OF TOM HANSON, THE ;
Or, Brave Endeavours Achieve Success ; a Story for
Boys.   By Firth Garside, M.A.   5s.   Illustrated.   Hand-
somely bound.

HARRY'S BIG BOOTS : a Fairy Tale, for " Smalle
Folke."   By S. E. Gay.   With 8 Full-page Illustrations and
a Vignette by the author, drawn on wood by Percival
Skelton.   Crown 8vo., handsomely bound in cloth, price 5s.
"Some capital fun will be found in ' Harry's Big Boots.'. . The illustra-
tions are excellent and so is the story."—*Pall Mall Gazette.*

ROSIE AND HUGH ; a Tale for Boys and Girls.
By Helen C. Nash.   1 vol., crown 8vo.   6s.
"In ' Rosie and Hugh' we have all the elements of fiction presented in
the best possible form to attract boys and girls.   Wholesome, pure, lively,
with here and there a dash of humour, the book is certain to be a favourite
with both parents and children . . . . . A cheerful, clever work."—*Morning
Post.*

SEED-TIME AND REAPING.   A Tale for the
Young   By Helen Paterson.   Crown 8vo.   5s.

FLORENCE OR LOYAL QUAND MEME.   By
Frances Armstrong.   Crown 8vo., 5s., post free.

MILES : a Town Story.   By the author of " Fan."
Crown 8vo., 5s.

Samuel Tinsley & Co., 10, Southampton St., Strand.